Th

by

Christoph Fischer

Create Space ISBN – 978-1505317305

Create Space ISBN – 1505317304

Cover design by Daz Smith of nethed.com

For my new Godson Rhys, and his
parents Liz and Andy
And

Dave 'Needles' Pearson

www.christophfischerbooks.com

Table of Contents

Part 1

Chapter 1

The tired, small hatchback hit a rock next to the edge of the road and came to an unexpected and abrupt stop. Erica had not seen the bulky thing hidden underneath the uncut grass. She switched off the engine and got out. There seemed no significant damage to her old banger but she couldn't care less right now, to be honest, and decided she would leave it parked here anyway. She must be close.

Quite frankly, she considered herself lucky to have made it this far; the roads had been bumpy and her car was in a dire condition, too. It wouldn't be much longer before it would have to be scrapped. Living in London she rarely needed it and had often been tempted to sell it anyway.

This was deepest Wales, the countryside - something that the Londoner in her had not seen for years and certainly hadn't missed. Poor phone reception, miles to the nearest supermarket with its supplies of cigarettes and bubbly: that's what the countryside meant to her.

She guessed the car was sufficiently off the road and out of the way. Who would come here, anyway? It was unlikely that two cars would find this remote corner of Wales at the same time, she reckoned. Erica looked around: not a living soul in sight, no houses or vehicles; she was totally off the beaten track. She could see no significant landmarks; all views were blocked by large trees and hedges. It was drizzling a little and although it was past lunchtime, there was mist that reminded her of early mornings. The wind had made the spring temperatures drop more than she had anticipated and she was chilly in her inadequate city clothing.

She searched her purse for the map, which her assistant Hilda had drawn for her. It seemed as if she was in the right place; there was the small path at the foot of the hill, and the two opposing gates leading to fields with horses and sheep. Since leaving her nearby B&B, all the road junctions she had come to had been easy to recognise and here was the little shoulder by the side of the road, where Hilda had recommended she should park the car.

She assured herself once more that it was the right path and then she psyched herself up for the walk up the steep hill. The tricky part, Hilda had explained, was finding the hidden gate, which would lead her to the man himself. However, Hilda didn't have pancreatic cancer and was not recovering from a course of chemo and so she had no idea how difficult it would be for Erica to walk up that hill. It seemed by no means the easy climb her assistant had called it. For all her recent goodness, that woman could drive her mad.

Erica looked at herself in the outside mirror of her car before getting ready to face the man. Her hair had not fallen out from the chemo but it had turned grey and made her look much older than she was. There were still crow's feet and wrinkles despite being facially bloated – it really wasn't fair; the worst of both worlds. People used to think of Erica as at least five years younger than she actually was, but now people thought she was five years older. Overnight it seemed, she had aged from 40 to 50 but given her current situation she would be lucky to reach 45. Additionally, she had lost a lot of weight, despite the effect that the steroids had had on her. With her mere 5' 4" frame, she looked tiny and felt thin and weak.

Only this man might be able to improve her chances and she desperately hoped the trip here would be worth it. If the man really was who Hilda thought, there was a slight chance for her. If she could make him speak to her, then she was sure she could persuade him to help - if he still possessed *those* powers. There suddenly seemed a lot of ifs.

She locked the car and began the climb up the tree-covered hill. Her trainers slid on the moist moss, her jeans too tight for some of the big steps she had to take. There was only a tiny trodden path, which seemed easy to lose sight of, curving its way upwardly through the trees. She was glad she had the map. Hilda deserved an award for organising this; if Erica ever made it back to her position at work she would make sure to find a way of compensating her, if she had anything left after she had paid the man.

Her assistant had come here a few days ago and had scouted the place out in the manner of a gifted detective. Hilda had been an angel the last few months with an uncalled for loyalty and devotion which Erica felt she didn't deserve. Erica cringed when she thought of the numerous times she had blown a fuse in the office and let out her life's frustrations on this

7

woman: she had complained about the coffee being too milky, the memos being too floral or the diary too busy. If only she had known how her life would play out, she would have made many decisions in different ways and definitely would have treated Hilda with more respect and humanity. Well, it was too late for regrets, she could only hope to make it right in the future, if she had one. For now it was time to keep going and move forward and rescue whatever she could.

A chicken wire ran parallel to the path, then some strong wooden fence panels replaced it that were so thickly overgrown with ivy that Erica would have missed seeing the gate itself, had it not been for the directions on the map.

To her surprise the gate was unlocked. A dog barked and howled from afar but it stayed at a safe distance. The noise was not very aggressive anyway and her guess was that this was a companion rather than a guard dog; a further indication that she was at the right place. She doubted that this spiritual guru called Arpan would have aggressive attack dogs around for protection: that would not be the style of someone so ostentatiously non-violent and serious. What she remembered about the man was admittedly extremely vague and distorted by what Hilda had told her.

He had made some headlines a long time ago and at the time, Erica had often seen his picture; if only she had paid more attention to current affairs. Her personal circumstances at the time had kept her pre-occupied and now she was unsure how the press had handled him. Hilda was of the opinion that this was a good thing, since Erica should meet him and find out for herself anyway. Arpan would probably not like to give such an unfavourable impression; Erica thought she remembered him as being very image orientated. He'd either maintain a soft and gentle outward image or would be far too cocky and confident; since the beginning of mankind, gurus had behaved as if they were invincible.

She reminded herself that she had to keep an open mind about this and that it was better to think the best of the man. After all, she had nothing more to lose.

Erica had to navigate between some very overgrown bushes until she came to a small clearing at last. A dome structure was at the other end of the clearing, made of wood and concrete and what looked like parts of camping tents. Solar panels, vegetable beds and free range animals populated the clearing: goats, chicken and sheep. She should have expected that. Green and new age living, she supposed.

"Arpan?" she called out. "Hello?"

An Alsatian came jumping out of the dome full of excitement and began to sniff and lick Erica's hand. He did not look like a puppy but he certainly behaved like one. She knelt down to stroke him gently. The dog wagged his tail excitedly and lay down on the ground, inviting her to rub his belly, and Erica happily obliged. What a happy little dog. She'd forgot how much fun dogs could be.

"Ashank, come back here!" a male voice called from inside the dome. "Come here!"

"Arpan?" Erica repeated shyly. "Hello, is that you, Arpan? I need to speak to you… please."

A young man, maybe 20 years old, slim, spotty and dressed in baggy, red and pink clothes, came briefly out of the dome and called the dog back. Ashank rolled on his side, jumped up and ran to his master. Before Erica could engage with him, the man had zipped the entrance to the dome shut. From what she had seen, his was not the voice she had heard, Erica was sure of it. The person who had called the dog from inside the tent sounded mature and older, much more like that of the Arpan she had heard about. Exactly how she had imagined him to be.

"I need to speak to you, Arpan. It's urgent," Erica called out again, unsure how best to proceed. She wished he would come out of the dome, so she could read his body language and figure out how to best 'work' him. Years in the advertising business had taught her how to handle these situations and she prided herself for her skills in that department. Him not coming out of the dwelling was its own kind of body language and dictated the rules of engagement; she would have to change them, break him down and transform this into a more intimate conversation.

"Go away. You're in the wrong place," the voice called out, sounding tired and slightly annoyed.

"Arpan, I need your help. Please talk to me!" she pleaded. "Hear me out. A few minutes of your time is all I ask of you. Please listen, and then I will go away."

9

"Who are you anyway?" the man asked, still not showing himself, but she thought she had seen a piece of the tent move. Perhaps he had seen her now and in her current fragile state that had to work in her favour. She looked positively ill and maybe this would appeal to his charitable side. To have done all the good things that he did in youth, he had to have some feelings and a heart. Even if he was a changed man now – as the abrupt stop to his healing practice implied - there had to be a little of his old self beneath the icy exterior, and she would try her damnedest to get to it.

"I'm very ill. You are my only hope now," she said calmly, eager not to overplay for sympathy.

"As I said: you've come to the wrong place," was the curt reply. "I can't help you."

"You have a gift, Arpan, I know you do. And I know you cannot let me die like this. You have a good heart, don't you? They once said that you were an 'Offering' to the world, that is the meaning of your name Arpan, isn't it? Even if you hide yourself away now, you have a responsibility to the world to share this gift. Save me, please!"

"I have responsibilities alright, but they are not to you or anybody else out there," Arpan replied in the manner of a sulky child. "You need to leave now."

"I beg you," Erica said, and sank to her knees. The sudden plunge hurt not only her knees but every other of her joints too. The muddy floor drenched her jeans, but she hardly cared.

"You seem familiar. You're not some journalist, are you? What did you say your name was?"

"Maria Miller," Erica lied. "So you really are Arpan," she added relieved and hopeful. She had found the right man, or rather, her assistant Hilda had. If she were religious, she would bless the Lord.

"I said no such thing," the man shouted back angrily. "I call myself Amesh. A different name altogether, a different man and a different life. One more suited to me. Please get up and leave."

"It doesn't matter what name you have. I'm dying, Amesh, so I don't have much time left to persuade you to help me."

"The man you're looking for is no more. I wish I could help you, but I simply can't. He disappeared with the name. Go

10

home and do the only thing you can do: make peace with your enemies, tell your loved ones how much they mean to you and sort out all of your affairs in a manner that will make you proud. If it is your time to die, you should not waste the gift of time by looking for miracles that didn't find you on their own. Not many have the opportunity to right their wrongs. Use it wisely."

"Maybe you're right," Erica said, after a few seconds of deliberation. "If it really is my time to die, I will. I have already begun the process of righting my wrongs, as you call it. I had given up all hope and had resigned myself to die. But then I found you and I seriously believe that found you for a good reason. Many others must have tried to find you and didn't succeed. If things are meant to be, then this meeting between us now might not be a coincidence, so please let's talk. Let me at least look at you. Let us stand face to face. Maybe it will help me so I can bury the illusion that you would have been the one man left on the planet able to save me."

She heard a whisper in the tent, then the young boy came out from under the dome and looked her up and down. He was slim but more muscled than what she had initially thought, not as tall as he had looked just moments earlier, blond dreadlocks and a beard hiding some of his spots, piercings, tattoos and a cocky walk. Although he had a young face, he carried himself like someone who had been through a lot and knew how to handle life. He was focused but not quite calm enough to carry it off completely convincingly.

"You don't have a microphone or anything, do you?" He asked and frisked her. He was not shy touching her. "Let me look into your backpack," he said and rummaged through it when Erica offered it to him without hesitation. All Erica had brought with her were pen and paper, some snacks and her purse.

"She's clean," he called out to the man still hiding inside.

"What does Amesh mean?" Erica asked. "If Arpan meant 'Offering', then surely Amesh must have a meaning. What is it?"

"Coward Boy," said the old voice.

She was shocked at that and fell silent.

At last the man himself stepped out of the tent, with the Alsatian dancing around him. "The name represents what I have become."

11

Amesh looked nothing like she had expected. He had shaved his beard off and also his long, dark, Jesus-like hair. Bold and haggard he was a shadow of his former self. At least 60 and looking every bit of it, his face seemed deflated, his shoulders were hunched and there was nothing left of the charismatic persona Arpan had once been. She could see why he had chosen Amesh as his new name, there was something timid about him. It suited him better than Arpan, 'the Offering', as he had been known.

"You see," Amesh said shrugging his shoulders. "Stripped off all the glamour and of all power! I'm just your regular woodland hermit, growing vegetables and talking to the trees."

A hint of recognition slipped across his face.

"You remind me of someone," he said, but Erica shook her head. "Well, maybe it is the disease you have that makes me think I know you," he added. "I spent years with it and have seen it in all of its shapes and forms. Are you sure we haven't met before?"

"I know we haven't," she said quickly.

"How did you even find me?" he asked, looking intensely at her as if scanning her thoughts while he was doing it. "It's quite worrying," he added. "I'll finally have to succumb to necessity and install security again. Can't you people simply leave me alone? It's been years since anyone has taken notice of me. I thought I was at peace at last."

"I'm sorry," she replied sheepishly. "I guess it was the right amount of desperation and luck. For what it's worth, I can assure you that the people who helped me wouldn't give out your secret easily."

"I should hope so. Not many have any clue as to where I live these days. Trust me, I will silence them myself as soon as I can," he said forcefully, but Erica didn't think he meant it.

"Well, now that you've seen me in my new earthly incarnation I hope you can go back to your life in peace, knowing that you didn't miss out on some miracle that was meant for you. You can tell that I'm not the man you're looking for." He opened his arms in a gesture of disclosure and even turned around for her to have a good look.

"What happened to Arpan?" she asked, hoping to play up to his vanity. As long as she kept him talking, she was building a rapport. The more he knew about her, the more likely he was to

12

feel sorry and change his mind. If he ever had the powers to heal pancreatic cancer with his hands, then that ability had to have stayed with him. As long a shot as this was, if he had done it once he had to be able to do it once more for her.

He shook his head. "As I've said, Arpan is no more. The world has transformed him and his gift, and it put me in his place."

"That's very cryptic. What's that actually supposed to mean?"

"You know, you sound just like a journalist," he said with a grin. "If I didn't see the disease in your face I would say you're here only looking for a scoop. Either way, what I said means simply that I don't have the powers that you seek."

"You healed hundreds of people," Erica insisted.

"That wasn't me; it was Arpan, 'the Offering'. He was something else, entirely. I cannot heal you, however much I wish I could," Amesh said resigned.

"You could at least try."

"Maria, you know nothing about me, about Arpan or about the so-called miracles. I indulged you by letting you see me, as you requested but I beg of you to leave now and to keep my location a secret. Arpan has given enough to the world, now it is time for Amesh to live his life to suit his needs."

"You can't give up on a calling like yours," Erica said with growing desperation.

"Amesh can and Arpan did, too. If you knew more you would probably understand."

"I have money, plenty of it, and I can get more, if that's what it takes," Erica blabbered in panic. She knew it was the wrong approach but she just couldn't help herself.

"Do I look like I need money?" Amesh said, shaking his head and pointing around him. "This is not the life of someone who wants lots of money - that should be very obvious to anyone."

"Actually, if I'm honest, it looks like the property of someone who could do with quite a lot of money." Erica contradicted. "It could buy you more living space, better isolation against rain and wind, to say the least, and security or a receptionist to help you out."

"I don't want any of that," Amesh said dismissively, "and I really don't need or want your money, thank you very much."

"Arpan took 50% of everything his patients owned," Erica said accusingly. "How does that fit in with what you are saying? For all his spirituality, Arpan did like the cash. Has it all gone? Looks like Amesh could do with a topping up his bank accounts to improve this place. At least get it safe for the next winter. I can help you if you help me."

"Arpan didn't 'like' the money, but the payment was an important and a very necessary part of the process," Amesh replied. "If the people who came to him weren't prepared to give this much for their life, then Arpan wasn't able to help them, just as western medicine couldn't help them. You need to value your life and the cost of keeping it."

Erica had to bite her tongue. Her natural distrust for miracle healers and un-scientific claims was ever-present but she mustn't alienate Amesh with her critical thoughts.

"If someone values their wealth above their health, then western medicine or *any* alternative measures can only slightly prolong their life," Amesh lectured her. "They are doomed, and nobody can stop the course of their destiny. People cheated Arpan and paid him only a fraction of what they were worth. When the disease then indeed didn't go away they asked for their money back, and Arpan returned all of those monies, without even charging them for his time, which they wasted. Every single person who didn't get cured was reimbursed. Many brought it onto themselves, I hasten to add."

"I get that you are retired for some reason or another and bitter with the world about something it did to you, but that doesn't necessarily mean that you're suddenly incapable of healing," Erica said. "Whatever it was that stopped you practicing at the height of your fame doesn't justify throwing away your gift. You mustn't let the newspapers and their hate campaigns get to you. You must at least try. Try on me to see if your powers are back. Please."

"You are so naïve," Amesh replied and sneered. "The work Arpan did was more complex than you will ever be able to comprehend. The newspapers and their treatment of him were not what stopped him; they were simply a symptom of the all underlying evil that stopped him: human nature and society. I

14

don't want to get into the whole thing. As Amesh, I'm happy now and I lead a life that suits me just fine. I have a right to enjoy it."

"But…" she began, but he interrupted.

"Enough said. I have asked you to leave on numerous occasions and you have refused to comply. You are trespassing on my property and I wish for you to leave now. Anuj will escort you of the premises," he said and, as if on command, the young man came towards her, followed by the excitable Alsatian; he took her by the elbow and led her away.

"Please, Anuj," Erica pleaded on their way to the gate. "Put in a good word with him for me. I'm desperate and I don't have much time. Here is my card. I'm staying at Woodlands B&B, which is not far from here."

Anuj took the card and put it in his pocket.

"Don't get your hopes up," he warned. "As Amesh, he is hurting and as Arpan, he hasn't seen a client since he retreated from the limelight years ago. We also don't have a phone or computer and I doubt that you will hear from him. Do as he says and get on with your life, or what is left of it. He doesn't play games and this is not a case of 'playing hard to get'. I agree with him, that your time is a gift to get your life in order. I can tell there is a lot for you to do. Trying to be saved is a selfish use of the little time you have left when there are many things you should be doing instead. Think of the things you have to do before your time is up. Think of the people around you and what they need: goodbyes, sorting of affairs… there is so much. When you come to think of it, I doubt that you really have time for us, don't waste it by holding out for an unobtainable miracle. Think of the things you need to do and the people that need you."

"Those people need me alive," Erica said. "If they care, they need me alive."

"You need to trust what he said. Amesh might only be a shadow of what Arpan was but he can still see into people's souls. It's like a psychic X-ray; he gets people with only one look. I'm only his apprentice but I too can see the disorder in your life that needs to be rectified. You carry hurt and anger with you. Your disease has prompted you to fast track those issues and requires you to sort them out. Look into your heart and you will find this to be true."

"Tell him I'll be waiting for your call," Erica said stubbornly, "Amesh must have seen my determination," she added just before Anuj closed the gate behind her.

Angrily she walked down the hill, slipped twice and fell over the root of a tree. She had a few scratches and skinned one of her knees. Since the chemo, her skin was so fragile and seemed to rip open at the slightest touch. She got into her car and tried to start it, but the engine would not spring to life. She tried and tried but gradually realised that she was stuck. Here, of all places. This couldn't have happened anywhere worse. There was nobody, no sign of civilisation, people, houses or even mobile phone reception. For a brief moment she contemplated going back up the hill but she feared Arpan and Anuj would see it as a fake excuse and that would in no way help her cause with those two, of that she was sure. They would help her with the car but it might put them off for good and then he would never agree to help her with her illness.

Her body was aching badly and her painkillers made her terribly tired, so she decided to take a little rest before making any further plans. She quickly nodded off in the driver's seat and slept for several hours. It was late afternoon when a knocking on her car window woke her. It was Anuj with the Alsatian.

"Nice try," Anuj said dismissively when she explained her predicament to him. "Don't think we'll be changing our mind because of a broken down car."

"I wouldn't dream of such a thing," she said. "Just tell me what you suggest I should do."

He nodded and said with a hint of sarcasm: "It's only a two mile walk from here to the next farm. I'm sure they'll let you call the rescue services. I'll draw you a map how to find them."

"Thank you," Erica said as gracefully as she could. "I'll do that then."

She took her backpack and followed his directions. The walk was definitely much longer than the two miles Anuj had promised. The thought occurred to her that she mustn't get lost or she would never get out of here alive. The lush green Welsh countryside here started to grow on her a little: the constant rain had at least one upside. She had heard her fanatic hiking colleagues say that one could go days without meeting anyone else in some of these 'off the beaten track' locations. Obviously that was what Arpan or Amesh had gone for and what had brought her into trouble. She had tempted fate by driving here in such an old banger, she knew that.

She had to sit down and rest several times as she kept running out of breath. The farm was abandoned when she got there. After what seemed like an eternity of resting on a garden bench, she was getting concerned. At this time of the year, the sun would set soon and she had to consider all of her options. She began to worry that no-one would come home to the farm and she had to make use of the little daylight that was left to get back to her car. She would rather sleep in her car than somewhere here as an intruder in a farm outbuilding. At least, she had some food and a blanket in her car, here she would be nothing but a trespasser again. When she got back to her Fiesta it was already pitch dark. It didn't take much for her to fall asleep again and despite the wildlife noises that she was unaccustomed to, she slept all the way through to sunrise.

Chapter 2

Something about the country air seemed to agree with Erica. She had not slept this deeply for ages. Her neck was a little stiff from the uncomfortable position she had slept in but it hardly mattered. She got to see a fantastic sunrise through the trees, a picturesque setting that was a welcome distraction from her current problems. A few grey clouds were scattered around the horizon but their colour display against the orange of the sun was nothing short of sensational. For a few precious moments she forgot her cancer and her pain – well, almost.

She stretched and had some cereal bars from her backpack, took her pain medication and got out of the car. She would have to ask Anuj and Amesh for help, at least ask them for directions to a different farm. She resented having to do this, she didn't want to come off as too needy and pushy, and most of all, she dreaded the uphill struggle ahead of her. As she was almost done with the taxing climb and was close to the gate she could hear the two men chanting. Apparently there was still some of Arpan's Eastern famous spiritual practice going on here. He may have retreated from the healing role but the lifestyle suggested he had not moved on to an entirely different world view. If he was still one of those people then there was far more hope for her to convince him than she had thought.

Erica waited discreetly outside the fence until the chanting had died down. Interrupting the men would not help their goodwill. Eventually it appeared that the men had finally stopped their singing and she walked through the gate quietly, trying to find out what they were doing now and if it was a good moment to attract their attention yet. The Alsatian found her but without barking this time. Before she could make her presence known he jumped up on her and joyously licked her face. Anuj came to investigate what the dog was up to and when he saw her he breathed a heavy sigh and motioned for her to come to the clearing.

"There was nobody at the farm," she explained as he cast her disparaging looks. "I need directions to somewhere else, then I promise to leave you alone. I'm very sorry about all this."

"I'll have a look at your car," Anuj offered, still without showing too much sympathy. Somehow she had expected to find more compassion from two spiritual men. "Give me the keys," he said and as soon as she had done, he left the compound.

Amesh looked at her with both, suspicion and compassion. How he did that was beyond her but he seemed to possess almost telepathic abilities – or did she begin to imagine things? She grasped the extent of his charisma and his magnetic abilities.

"Come inside and lie down while you're waiting," he said rather abruptly and led the way into the dome. The interior was surprisingly spacious. She had only seen the front but the place extended further into the woods with several alcoves on either side, all big enough to accommodate a bed or a desk. The floor was made of concrete, although it was not perfectly flat and was covered with old and worn out rugs. The back wall seemed to be made entirely of concrete, whereas some of the side walls seemed to consist of a mixture of wicker and plaster. The 'walls' were painted in different colours and had obscure drawings on them. There was a lead from the generator outside, a little wood burner and a fire stove.

"Lie down on the mattress and close your eyes," Amesh instructed her. She happily obliged, the climb had taken it out of her and she was more than grateful for a little rest and comfort. The mattress he had chosen for her was in one of the alcoves and it smelled a little fragrant; the two men clearly used soap sparingly, probably to save the environment. The smell provoked her nausea at first but then the feeling settled and she began to relax.

Soon after that she felt Amesh's hands on her shoulders, pressing her firmly into the floor. The warmth of his - well what could she call it, aura, presence - radiated powerfully through her body, making every cell and every inch of her skin feel strong and vibrant; her mind lost itself, almost as if in a trance. She wanted to cry, it felt that good. The weight that seemed to drag her down every minute of the day since she had been diagnosed with cancer was falling off her in large chunks and she felt as if she was floating on air. She couldn't hold it together any longer and burst into a fit of uncontrollable sobs. She couldn't believe how affected she was. Her body was shaking as if she was connected to an electric current. Gradually the sensation began to ebb and a calm after the emotional storm set in. She felt good, really good even; too good to move in any case and she didn't want to change anything about this unless she absolutely had to. This was pure heaven.

"How are you feeling?" he asked.

This could not be. His voice came from the other end of the room but she could still feel his hands on her shoulder. She opened her eyes and looked behind her but he was not there. The sensation of his hands on her shoulders only now began to disappear. She looked in astonishment at Amesh who sat in a yoga pose in the corner as if she wasn't there. Too exhausted to question any of this she let her head sink back down and fell into a comfortable semi sleep.

After a good ten minutes had passed, Anuj came into the dome and brought her at last fully back into the reality of the room.

"I fixed your car," was all he said.

"What was wrong with it?" Erica asked

"Not much," Anuj said matter of factly. "Your car probably picked up on you not wanting to leave here and decided to help," he added with a wink. She couldn't make out whether it was meant as sarcasm or whether he was for real.

"Nonsense," she said and shook her head.

"If you don't believe in the power of the mind and in energy that is not measurable by conventional means then you really shouldn't have come here in the first place," Amesh added.

"Oh. I believe in what you do," she said, directing her comment straight at Amesh. "Especially now that I felt your hands on me while you were metres away: that was clear proof of your abilities. But to kick start a car with your own hands, as Anuj has just implied, that's a bit much to believe. Tell me, what was wrong with it? Are you a mechanic? I need to know so I can have it fixed by a garage."

"You're free to believe as you will or must, but a garage won't find anything wrong with it. Here are your keys anyway," Anuj said. "Bon voyage!" and with that he left the dome.

"I've had all kinds of massages: Reiki, Shiatsu and lord knows what since I contracted cancer," she said, still laying down. "Nothing has ever been this powerful. I'm starting to really

20

believe that you have a gift to heal and I'm convinced more than ever that you can help me. That you can save me."

"And yet, you refuse to believe that my disciple could heal your car?" Amesh said with a sceptical look.

"I'm afraid so," she confessed.

"You people amuse me with your scepticism."

"I've had to make a huge leap of faith; even going to my first Yoga lesson was a big step. I'm a fast learner. I can see you're using fengshui colours and schemes on your wall, I heard the chanting and I saw a little of your morning Tai Chi. I've tried some of these things myself recently and I'm trying to keep up with it all," she said. "Certain things are just a little hard to accept when you're taught from early childhood that only science counts."

Amesh laughed. "I don't practice Tai Chi. It's Qi Gong, but I guess that's just a name to you. I've met many people like you over the years," he reassured her. "People doubt and block the help they're getting, unless they can explain it. They don't have faith, but they need it to get better. That is why Arpan asked his clients for half of their wealth. He probably should have taken 100%. He needed them to value his services, to convince themselves that it was worth it. It made the ones who decided to go for it commit completely. It changed their attitude, which was usually part of the original problem and their disease."

"You must understand how those exorbitant fees made you enemies, especially amongst those with the lowest income," Erica replied as she stood up from the mattress.

"I agree that for some of the richer clients the fee was something they could easily afford. Yet, trust me, in the mind of the rich, who can afford almost anything, half of their wealth is just as unimaginable. Money is an addiction. The more you have, the more you need. 50% from a millionaire is a serious threat to his sense of security and even his existence, possibly even more so than it is to someone of a lower income. Maybe Arpan could have implemented a more sophisticated system but he never anticipated this much interest and media hype when he first started."

"What about the poor, though? How could he ask them for that much?" she said, almost angrily.

"Material things are nothing, you cannot take them with you beyond the grave; however, what you have become, your soul and your essence - all that can transcend. The only thing Arpan felt comfortable asking for was money because it means nothing. If his clients could meet him at least half way, then they had a fighting chance that the treatment would work."

"And it did work," Erica said enthusiastically. "What on earth happened that persuaded you to stop?"

"I will answer that another day, Maria. Now tell me: would you be willing to give me 50 % of all of your earthly possessions for a taste of my powers?"

"I'd give you 100% to live," Erica said. "Who in their right frame of mind wouldn't?"

"You'd be surprised how short sighted people can be even in the face of death. They're happy to bargain with their own death, desperate to hold on to a little bit of luxury. They think they can cheat and have everything and get away with it. I'll take you at your word though. If I should heal you, I want 100% of all your assets. Everything. You need to bring me bank statements, pay slips, shares and all monetary information that there is. I need you to swear under oath that you haven't hidden anything from me, although I must warn you that I'm pretty good at seeing it in people's eyes if they are lying. Plus, you need to sign a non-disclosure agreement that you will never speak to anyone about me and this treatment. If you're not healed I will reimburse you, but you mustn't tell a living soul where I live and what I do."

"I was told that this is what you used to do, so I have already brought all of these documents you need with me. Everything you asked for is in the B&B. I can fetch it now and come back right away."

"I only asked you a question. You need to go away and think very hard about it. The treatment is an ordeal and will change you. I need to meditate a good deal on this before I can make the commitment, Maria. I haven't worked on anyone like I did this afternoon on you for a very long time. That had nothing to do with Arpan, even if it felt a bit like him. I'm astonished to see you having this much desperation and this much faith in me; you and your scientific mind, I mean. I, on the other hand, have still some catching up to do. When you came here, I felt for the first time in many years that powerful sense of a calling that I

22

used to have. I must ask my higher self if I am ready to answer it."

"Meditate all you like," Erica said, "but I don't need to think about it twice. I'll fetch all of my documents from the B&B all the same and come right back here. Hopefully by then you too will have made up your mind."

"For me, the situation is slightly more complex than a simple yes or no. I have implications to think about that you would know nothing of. Please don't assume that I will decide to help."

"I'll go and get my stuff in any case. I want to be ready."

"Go ahead, but note that I am not making any guarantees of any kind right now. However, should we both decide to proceed, the other thing that I need you to do for this to work is to throw away all of your medicine. I want your body to be clean and a pure vessel of my energy only."

"But you have not committed to the healing," Erica protested. "If you turn me down I'll be left with nothing."

"It's your choice," he said coolly. "Take it or leave it. Think about it and try to understand why I'm asking this of you. You seem an intelligent woman, I'm sure you can figure it out."

"Yes, I get it, total commitment," Erica said and nodded.

"Something like that," Amesh replied with a grin. "You do need to leave now, I must meditate. Come back tomorrow. You must sleep on it at least once before you part with this much money. Now that you've met me, meditate on the best course of action for you. And a warning: know also that once I begin working on you, your western pain relief will no longer provide you with the comfort and escapism that you're accustomed to. You need to make that decision consciously. If you're prepared to make those sacrifices and to put your trust in me completely we have a fighting chance of making this work. It will hurt, it won't be easy and it will take a lot from you in every possible sense."

Erica nodded absentmindedly. Amesh turned away and took an obscure yoga position and held it without showing any sign of acknowledging her presence. She waited for an official dismissal but gave up and went to her car. She couldn't believe the unexpected spring she felt in her step on the way down. Over all the heavy talk about commitment she had not even noticed how light and alive she still felt after the treatment he'd given her.

The man was a miracle worker, even if that was difficult to accept with her scientific mind. To her amazement, the car sprang to life and took her back to the B&B without the slightest hint of a problem. Maybe she was just imagining it, but the car seemed to drive much smoother than it ever had.

The B&B that Hilda had found for her was a pretty, large white stone cottage which had several modern extensions added to the main building, with boring magnolia walls and large windows and French doors. To get to her room, Erica had to walk from the car park past the kitchen window and as if she had been waiting, the owner, Mrs Jones, saw her, waved and came barrelling towards her in no time.

Erica took some time to placate the woman.

"I've been worried sick, Miss Miller," she said excitedly. "I didn't know if I should call the police or the rescue services with you having gone missing. What on earth happened to you? Where have you been? Are you alright?"

A busybody if Erica had ever seen one. Mrs Jones was over 50, had untameable, greying, ginger hair, was chubby and had the most intrusive, greedy green eyes that looked even larger through her glasses. Her apron accentuated the bulge of her stomach most disadvantageously and her eager smile couldn't hide her bossy rather than caring attitude.

"I stayed with friends," Erica said evasively.

"Friends?" Mrs Jones asked with emphasised surprise. "I didn't know you had friends in Wales. You said you were here on vacation and to see our beautiful nature. Who are your friends? Do they live nearby?" she added and grabbed Erica's hand as if to make sure her guest wouldn't run away before answering to her. Erica had moved backwards during this interrogation and looked away in discomfort. She couldn't think of a good enough excuse or cover story and was lucky to be saved by Mrs Jones inability to shut up.

"I wish you had told me you were staying out overnight," the woman filled the short silence immediately. "It's not a problem, but of course I had no idea what was going on. I was awake all night worrying about you," she added accusingly.

24

"I'm so sorry for the inconvenience," Erica said at last, without making eye contact. "I promise that won't happen again."

Mrs Jones sighed heavily for effect. "Well, never mind. As long as you know that I lock the front door at 10pm unless I'm otherwise notified and you'll need to use the backdoor at the end of the extension to get in after that."

Erica nodded and then she went to her room where she sent a text to Hilda to inform her of her progress and to warn her of the upcoming financial transactions.

Although she felt fresh and invigorated, she decided to lie down on her bed and stretch out. Within minutes she fell asleep and slept all the way through until the next morning.

Chapter 3

Erica had a rude awakening when she realised that her pain, the lethargy and the heaviness weighing on her mind and body had all returned overnight; the brief interlude of relief and all feelings of freshness and lightness she had gotten from yesterday's healing had stopped abruptly with the sound of her alarm. Additionally, she felt as if she had the worst hangover of her life. Nauseous and discombobulated, she lacked a sense of purpose and direction; a splitting headache added to her regular pain and her first instinct was to grab the bottle of painkillers and get comfortably numb.

Would Amesh notice if she took just one tablet to take the edge off? Would he really be able to tell? Or would it in some way really interfere with his healing? His rule of cutting out western medicine and the tablet regime that her doctor had prescribed seemed to be just another part of the 'total commitment' he was asking for. She decided that she could not afford to risk the effectiveness of his healing, should he decide to work on her. He seemed to have a sense of knowing, a telepathic skill of some sort. Anuj had warned her of this and Erica surmised that Amesh might at the very least be able to read her body language. He was not like the many people she had met through work whom she regularly tricked and deceived effortlessly. She forced herself to leave all the bottles of pills untouched.

Hilda had told her that Amesh not only asked his clients to stop taking all medication but demanded that they throw them away before treatment started. Not taking pills was one thing, but prior to his confirmed commitment she couldn't possibly let go of them. However, such a gesture might impress him and win him round. If she met him and he could tell that she had not disposed of them she might risk losing her chance with him altogether. She decided that the best course of action was to hand all of her pills over to him at the first opportunity, even before he had a chance to ask her. She would surrender them and let him have complete control. He would then see her commitment and obedience – she guessed that was what he was looking for.

She was a little annoyed that the effect of Amesh's healing had worn off overnight: a glimpse of what life felt for the healthy.

For few years prior to the cancer, she had never felt good physically. Her excessive smoking and drinking and the complete lack of exercise had always made her feel uncomfortable in her body. Yesterday's sensations had been a unique experience and one she instantly craved to repeat. This morning her hair needed a wash, her skin felt tight and spotty, her teeth needed cleaning and her back ached from the uncomfortable mattress she had slept on. Everything that Amesh had taken away had returned with a vengeance.

Fortunately the work Anuj had done on her car proved longer lasting than that. The car started without any problems and the short journey to the dome went as smooth as if she were driving a new car. She parked it in the same layby, a little more carefully this time. Walking up that hill showed Erica how out of shape her body was. Yesterday this had been a dreadful ordeal, today it seemed even worse. She couldn't help but feel a flicker of doubt again.

"The treatment you gave me yesterday was fantastic but it didn't last," she told Amesh when she saw him outside the dome. He looked fresher than yesterday and infused with life. "I'm feeling as poorly as I did yesterday, no, actually I feel worse, if I'm completely honest," she added. "Would you care to explain that to me?"

Amesh smiled as if she had complimented and not questioned him.

"Good," he replied cheerfully. "What I did yesterday was not the 'famous treatment'. It was a temporary relief and was never meant to last. As for the real thing, that won't make the cancer go away overnight either. The pain you're feeling right now is a sign that my healing yesterday initiated a response. Your body and the cancer felt attacked and like beasts in the jungle they will fight back furiously. I will need to weaken the disease in your body many more times before it loses its strength and finally succumbs to my powers. Be prepared for some tough times ahead."

Erica stared at him blankly as the concept of even more pain – and without any pills – sank in. She pulled herself together and straightened up.

"Here are the financial documents," she said and handed him a large document wallet. "And here are my pain killers and the rest of my medication regime. I thought it would be best to hand them directly to you, so you know they have all gone."

"Your word would have been good enough," he said. "I would know if you took them. I can feel them in my own blood when I treat people. Anuj, take a look at the documents for me please while I prepare Maria for the treatment."

He handed the file over to his disciple and then took Erica outside. He went through a ritual of breathing exercises and made her stand in all kind of odd poses, telling her to concentrate on energy flowing from one part of her body to another. She had tried exercises like these a few times herself, had even borrowed DVDs on energy meridians, but they had never worked for her. Anything this man did to her sent her spinning into a high and she felt invisible energy running warmly through her body.

"The documents are fine," Anuj told Amesh in the middle of the session. "I have the papers for her to sign."

"Are you ready for it, Maria?"

Erica was in such an altered state of mind, she could hardly make sense of her surroundings. She nodded all the same and signed the papers when Anuj put them in front of her.

"Amesh has become Arpan again," Anuj said triumphantly, but the man himself shook his head and led Erica back inside the dome where a massage table had been positioned in the centre of the room. He left the room for a little while, and then he came back in a striped and multi-coloured robe that was reminiscent of a freedom flag. He switched a sound system on that played calming, ambient music and handed Anuj ceremoniously a syringe with a green liquid.

"I will give you the first injection now," she heard the apprentice say, but her thoughts kept floating back and forth between understanding and confusion, alertness and delirium. She felt happy and safe and somehow her arm extended and offered itself to the needle as if it was the most natural thing in the world. After her run of chemo treatments, she was more than used to needles by now.

At first she felt nothing but shortly after Anuj had pulled the needle out she felt a burning sensation in her veins. It was not painful, but it was far from pleasant. She began sweating and shaking as if suffering from a fever. Only now did she notice that she had been strapped to the table and unable to free herself.

"Stay calm," Amesh/Arpan said to her, "your body will soon settle." He positioned himself behind her and put his hands on her shoulders, like he had done the day before. The effect was not at all the same, though. It felt violent and painful today, exactly like the medicine in her veins began to feel now, too. Erica screamed and cried out in pain, her body jerked with convulsions. The torture seemed to last for a very long time. When the worst of the pain receded and her shaking began to cease, the pain in her shoulders began to turn into a warm feeling and into a sensation of physical force and strength. It felt as if her muscles were growing and an unprecedented power was given to them, a feeling that began to radiate through the rest of her body with the flow of her circulating blood. Her mind could hardly keep up with the sensations flooding through her, the closest she could come to making sense of it was that her body had suddenly an armour of iron, she had been given supernatural powers and her veins were full of the essence of life. She rejected the ideas as ridiculous but it couldn't change her experience or take away the images in her mind.

After what seemed an eternity of floating, Arpan moved his hands over her body and performed a series of odd movements, as if he was painting something on her skin or sprinkling her with spices. She was fully clothed, so how she could feel his hands directly on her skin made no sense to her. He pushed down on parts of her body so intensely, she thought his fingers had actually gone through her skin and he was taking the cancer out of her body manually cell by cell. At last his hands settled back on her shoulders and then he told her to open her eyes. She was shell-shocked to hear his voice once again from across the room while she could still feel his hands on her shoulders. She turned her head around but he was really not standing behind her, nobody was.

"How... I mean... I thought..." she tried to express her amazement but the words would not come.

"Don't speak," he commanded in a firm but soft voice. "Let the feelings ebb naturally, you will know when to get up."

It seemed to take a long time before she came back from her 'trip'-like trance.

"Oh my God," she sighed eventually. "What was in that syringe?"

"I cannot tell you that," Arpan said.

Right now she didn't really care, she just couldn't believe that anything was able to give her such sensations. She had had her share of illegal thrills and artificially and synthetically produced highs but nothing had ever been like this.

He left the room for a minute and came back in his regular outfit.

"Are you reverting to Amesh now or are you Arpan for good?" she asked, looking at his clothes.

"The clothes don't make me Amesh or Arpan," he replied. "Time and your faith will tell you who I am. You can call me any name you like, I won't be offended."

"Of course you've always been Arpan to me," she said.

"That should be helpful in what we are doing," he replied. "How did you find the treatment and how are you feeling now?"

She described the sensations and images she had experienced over the last two hours in detail to him and Arpan nodded, but he never commented or indicated what he thought about them.

"I'm not sure how to put it in words what I'm feeling right now," Erica explained. "I've kind of become normal again, as in 'no longer high' but also as in 'no longer sick'. It's as if my body has found itself. Obviously the cancer has brought me out of sync with myself and interfered with everything that went on in my body. I'm more or less pain free and together. Will this last now, or will I feel bad again later?" she asked fearfully.

"It depends largely on your specific cancer cells," Arpan replied. "What you're feeling is what most patients described they experienced after the first injection, too. There is no way of telling how your cancer will react to this, though. You must imagine your cancer like a regular person who is only trying to live. We have attacked it twice now. Like human beings, some cancers fight until their last breath, whereas others will decide it isn't worth their time and give up without much resistance. I don't have a clear sensation yet about your cancer and what colours it may show us. Tomorrow, we both will know more about it, and it will affect how we proceed from there. You should probably go home and rest now. Do you have anyone with you who can look after you, family or friends?"

"No," she replied. "I don't."

30

"You should have someone who can take care of you, if needed," Arpan said. "You may go through quite an ordeal."

"I'm staying at the Woodlands B&B for the duration of this treatment. I sense the woman who runs it would quite like to know what I'm doing, so accepting her help would be a last resort. I knew in advance that I would have to sign the non-disclosure document, so I came alone," Erica explained.

"Well, look after yourself then," Arpan said, took her arm and simply walked her to the gate. Walking down the hill was easy, once again, which worried her a little. Yesterday the awakening from this ease had been terrible. What should she expect this time? And having an overbearing busybody around would make things only worse.

Chapter 4

Erica got to the B&B still feeling good. Once again she had to walk past the kitchen window where the nosy owner was doing the dishes. This time however she knew better than to look in and quickened her step to get to her room without having to make small talk or be questioned about her stay any further by the intrusive Mrs Jones. Erica got to her room before the woman caught up with her and once the door was closed, the expected knocking never materialised. Maybe the woman could take a hint after all. Erica was in no mood to talk to anyone right now. All she could think of was the treatment and she was not allowed to speak about it. Well, she would speak about it, but not with people in the locality who could upset Arpan in his isolation. She had promised him that and she took that part of her commitment very seriously. She would do nothing that could harm or upset him. However, she needed to talk to Hilda about it.

"How did it go?" Hilda wanted to know.

"Pretty intense really but I think he is truly onto something."

"I told you," Hilda said cheerfully.

"He's very weird, though," she continued. "One minute he's down to earth and speaks like a normal person, and then the next he puts on this arrogant guru persona. I've never experienced anything like it before; you know I've met my fair share of alternative healers but he is different. He's a really fascinating man and I wish I knew more about him: his fame, his background and everything else."

"You have all the paper cuttings, don't you? That should be more than enough," Hilda said, sounding hurt.

Erica sighed.

"Yes, that's true to some degree, but you only gave me a few about his famous success stories. There must have been much more to it. I remember some of the stuff in the papers at the time, about law suits and the money, I wish I had paid more attention to it, or researched it properly before coming here. I have no Wi-Fi here to check it out."

"Erica, don't burden yourself with any of that," Hilda pleaded. "Please, relax and let him do his magic. Think about it:

32

you'll come through this alive after all! What's the point of all this investigating and worrying? You felt something amazing, like hundreds of other people have in the past and you're going to live!" she promised.

"I think I really might," Erica said, only realising the strength of her faith as she said it. "Who would have thought, a cynical woman like me being cured by a healer?"

"Did he buy the fake paper work?" Hilda asked, a little more concerned and business like now. "I'm worried sick about that, you know. Did you really have to lie to him?"

"You know, I had to," Erica said annoyed. "And I'm only lying about the name, the rest is authentic. He will get all the money I promised him, I'm just retaining my anonymity and that is definitely worth the risk."

"I hope you know what you're doing," Hilda said. "That man is powerful and not to be trifled with. People with gifts like his often are psychic as well and can see through lies and deceit."

"I know, he told me all about how he would know if I ever lied to him. Anyway, I'm a little concerned about what I am going to do now that he has taken all of my pain killers. He gave me a short treatment yesterday and the after effects were very painful and violent. I was so tempted to keep some, but I believe him that he would feel it if I did."

"You be careful," Hilda warned her. "It's more than the painkillers that could become a deal breaker. His psychic or spiritual powers are well known. Our fake documents may be immaculate and perfect but that man senses things. For heaven's sake, if he can sniff cancer through your skin, then he should be able to tell a real name from a fake name. It might not be too late to come clean and appeal to his sense of justice and he may respond to that better than you think."

"Would he have treated me if he had figured me out?" Erica wondered. "He did it, that's the main point. Maybe he knows and is compassionate enough to forgive me. If he doesn't know then I won't have to worry."

"That man is your last and only chance, your last desperate shot at survival. Don't be stupid and risk being found out and dumped as a patient before his healing is complete. It's not worth it."

"If he finds out now who I am he might not finish the treatment. I'm stuck on the path I've chosen. We discussed it, and it seems to have worked. Let's leave it at that," Erica tried to end the conversation.

"Honesty is the best policy with people like him," Hilda insisted. "I know you're used to deception, game play and politics, but people like Arpan don't operate that way."

"I'm getting very tired all of a sudden," Erica said and it wasn't a lie.

"Don't you hang up on me," Hilda said, not believing her.

"Ow!" Erica swore under her breath. Out of nowhere she had an intense headache and a shooting pain running down her spine. "Ow... oh my... Hilda, I'm sorry, I really have to go, I feel awful," and with that she hung up and doubled over on her bed with terrible stomach cramp. Somehow she made it to the toilet and threw up, but then the cramp worsened and she had to sit down and hold the small plastic rubbish bin between her legs. Everything was violently shooting out of her body and she began to rock back and forth on the toilet seat as wave after wave of nausea rolled over her.

Exhausted she fell onto her bed an hour later, sweaty and clammy and totally deflated. The pain in her back was still there and felt very much like a bad flu. Fortunately her headache had receded, if only she wasn't too exhausted to appreciate it.

She drifted off but at midnight she woke up, starving, yet too nauseous to eat anything. This was how she imagined heroin withdrawal to be like; she felt terrible.

Laying on her bed she thought about Arpan and tried to remember what she knew. Back when he was a minor celebrity he had been so superior and so arrogant in photographs and on TV. From the little she had taken notice of, she had been under the impression that he suffered from a god complex: to call oneself a 'Blessing' or an 'Offering' - that had to be an ego trip. She had been surprised to find that he called himself something as extreme as 'Coward Boy' now, a long way down from 'Offering'. What had happened to this man that he could fall from grace, not only in the eyes of others but also in his own estimation? That he had a gift, there could be no doubt, and he seemed to know it too. Besides the healing though, there was something hugely fascinating, something that got her obsessively curious. What was the man behind the façade really like?

She knew his real name and his life story from the time before he became a healer; not many people shared this knowledge with her. He'd been a translator for the patent office in London before he had his first experience with alternative therapies. Keen on Yoga, he had taken time out to train as a yoga teacher in Thailand and India, gone to several Buddhist retreats and spent time in Japan, learning Reiki and Shiatsu. She recalled that he was qualified in several martial arts as well as acupuncture. According to Hilda's research the man had done so much, Erica was not sure if she remembered everything correctly. The fact was, he had done a lot of different things and changed his name several times before he discovered the 'elixir'. When her life had first collided with his, he had acted under his last civilian name and so she never made the connection with the famous healer Arpan, who by then had 'withdrawn' or retired anyway.

And why should she have made that connection? Erica never believed in any of the 'alternative medicine humbug'. She smoked, drank like a fish with her London pals and had enjoyed the occasional recreational illegal substance. Blessed with an overactive metabolism, she had ever had issues with body fat or body image and could eat almost anything she liked. Going to the gym might have given her some definition and shape but men always seemed to like her despite the fact that she did not exercise, they were content with her pretty face and never complained about her figure. Makeup could cover the unhealthy look of her skin if needed and the demands of her work-centred lifestyle simply didn't allow time for exercise. Although she lived relatively close to her work in Canary Wharf, commuting still took time every day; she worked long hours and then participated in more out of hours office politics in the pub. Erica had her life mapped out for her. She'd been a ruthless career woman, successful and promising, and until she was diagnosed with this inoperable pancreatic cancer there was nothing wrong with her life.

At 44 the verdict had been surprising. As consequence of her chain smoking, lung cancer would have been understandable; ovarian or breast cancer that claimed childless women like her early in life could have been a possibility, but pancreatic cancer, that was seriously uncalled for. It was one of the nastiest you could get, usually undetectable until it was too late and consequently with one of the smallest hopes for survival.

What smoker and consumer of unhealthy foods like her didn't have some kind of regular stomach pain? How could she have guessed that it was cancer? Sitting at her desk all day was bound to bring back pain, so instead of wasting her time with a doctor, she organised herself prescription strength painkillers and got Hilda to find her a more comfortable office chair. Erica had sat through a lot of pain before she started to get worried. Too busy during the day to take notice and too drunk in the evenings, she had waited far too long.

Stage four, as the hospital consultant explained to her, was beyond hope. The generous health plan provided by her employer could do little more than allow for more luxurious hospital accommodation with gourmet meals; it offered her a choice of treatment options but none of them would do more than delay her death by a few months. She had seriously considered not bothering with any of it but life, once threatened, seemed suddenly precious enough for her to give up smoking and to cling to the few extra days on Earth she might gain from the torture that was her treatment. However, the chemo made her feel so bad, she couldn't take it and gave up after the first course: she was too much of a wimp to power through it.

Her friends were not the type to stand by her through pain and illness and she found herself all alone in hospital and despairing over the pain and isolation. Busy London socialites and yuppies, as most of her so-called friends were, dropped her as soon as she had stopped working and coming out drinking with them in the evenings.

Erica hardly had time to catch up with the new harsh reality. She was stunned that the only person who stuck with her was her company assistant, Hilda. The 50 odd year old grey mouse that obediently did as she was told and whom Erica had treated despicably on more than one occasion, whom she had used to let off steam and anger, whom she had bossed around unnecessarily and about whom she had hardly ever asked a personal question. This unexpected loyalty and friendship was her first encounter with a miracle.

Hilda showed up at her hospital bed almost daily, brought the personal mail directed to her company address, magazines etc. and kept her abreast the office politics and new developments in the industry.

After the first course of chemo, Erica thought she was going to die because of her exhaustion and general weakness; she thought that it would finish her off quicker than even the cancer itself. At this point, Hilda introduced her to a brand new world. An acupuncturist successfully helped reduce Erica's pain levels and a Reiki master had made her feel wonderful in an hour's worth of not touching her.

"I must be desperate," she joked to Hilda. "To allow this superstitious humbug into my flat as a diversion is one thing, but to actually start to believe in it – that's something else."

"This is just the beginning," Hilda said enthusiastically. "I have some more tricks up my sleeve."

And she had. A Feng Shui master re-arranged the furniture in Erica's flat, got her to have the walls painted in different colours, de-cluttered the place for her and brought in some ornaments that would provide additional strength and health.

"Go ahead, I have nothing left to lose," Erica said when Hilda had first suggested all those changes. "I can't take the money with me and I have nobody to leave it to. I might as well see if it does me any good. If it doesn't, then the money will at least go to people who tried."

Whether it was the idea of combatting the cancer, the attention and sudden friendship with Hilda or whether the spiritual stuff was actually real, she didn't know. Erica felt an improvement and was so grateful for it that she saw the acupuncturist and the Reiki healer regularly. She was impressed with the power of what to her was quite obviously a placebo effect. The mind could do some pretty amazing stuff if it wanted to.

Then Hilda came up with information about Arpan.

"I won't have anything to do with him," Erica said adamantly when her assistant mentioned the name. She was sitting on her sofa with a hot water bottle, with nothing more than a dressing gown on. "He is where I draw the line. He's not real. I remember him and his absolute ego trip. No way. Wasn't there something controversial about him too? I can't think what it was, but there was a huge discussion about him."

"I know," Hilda agreed quietly. She took off her coat and rummaged in her handbag. "You should humour me though, and take a look at these articles that I printed off for you. His track record is incredible. If I were you, this is what I would be trying. Controversial or not, read these and tell me you're not tempted."

"What good would it do? Hasn't he stopped practising? I'm sure I remember that part," Erica pointed out.

"I know people," Hilda said with a suggestive move of her eyebrows. "I may be able to track him down for you. Everyone, however hard they try to hide, leaves a trail, and I might have the right connections to sniff him out."

"Not him, no," Erica said.

"Why? If you had one shot at all, he would be the one to take. Pancreatic cancer is the only thing he claimed to cure. To me that makes this a no brainer."

"I don't trust him. I've seen him on TV and in the papers. Something is off about that man," Erica had insisted and no begging from her assistant could change her mind.

"Well, I shall leave the cuttings here on the table," Hilda said when it was time to go. "I better be going home. Promise me to at least think about it."

Erica shook her head but during her next sleepless night she opened the file and had to admit that there was something compelling in them. Twenty odd years ago, when Arpan had been famous, Erica had dismissed the stories as a clever but definite con trick and as a fabricated myth. These magazine articles showed perfectly normal people, bankers, doctors and politicians, sensible, trustworthy and reliable witnesses as far as she was concerned, all vouching for the man and his abilities. Some of his former clients disclosed their entire medical history, hospital letters and scan results from all stages of the disease prior to seeing Arpan, followed by documentation from after they had been treated by Arpan. The scans after the treatment showed no traces of the cancer. The sheer number of patients with the same unbelievable stories spoke for itself. Erica had always been certain that Arpan's success had been a well organised trick, the product of some kind of mix-up of hospital records, of a computer fault or mass hysteria, but after reading these articles she was no longer so sure. The patients came from all walks of life and were not just gullible and easily hypnotised new age hippies; the results initially came from all corners of Britain but rapidly flowed in from the rest of Europe and the US as well.

Against her better judgement Erica began to feel a smallest vestige of hope. The weeks since her diagnosis had been hell: full of negativity, self-pity, anger and despair, the physical ordeal, the after effects of the chemo, the continuous pain, the erratic bowel movements and the ever present nausea. She felt constantly miserable, and only with the additional expensive help of alternative and massage therapies could she obtain a bearable level of existence.

Now Hilda promised her contact with Arpan and with it at least a slim chance of a rescue, not merely a lessening of the symptoms. She did not want to let that hope in, it was too tempting and too dangerous. What if nothing came off it? If she attempted to climb out of it, the fall back into the darkness of her misery would be too much to bear. No, she mustn't get carried away she told herself and never engaged when Hilda brought the matter up. Hilda however kept pressuring her.

"Why are you so insistent on this?" Erica asked once during a telephone conversation between her and her assistant. "You've only worked for me for four years during which I haven't been particularly kind to you. How is it that you do everything you do for me? Are you a Saint, or do you need to make amends for something else in your life?"

Hilda laughed. "You may have been harsh with me sometimes, but you were a much better person to work for than your predecessor. We shared our working life for a long time and you and I both have been living for our work, haven't we? I can't help but care for you and your wellbeing."

Now it was Erica's turn to laugh. "You're suffering from Stockholm Syndrome darling," she giggled.

"I know you're sceptical but you have nothing to lose and everything to gain," her assistant continued. "I know roughly where the man lives these days. It will be easy to find him and at least speak to him."

"No, I couldn't," Erica replied and let it lie, but she went over the articles several more times, her resistance gradually fading. The distinct possibility of success continually frightened her and she didn't want to get her hopes up over something so dubious, yet she found that she was only human and couldn't help but to pin her hopes onto this man.

At last she gave Hilda permission to enquire on her behalf. The longer she waited for an answer, the deeper her desperation grew. Damn that woman for making her vulnerable to disappointment once again. Life for Erica had only just officially shut down; she had accepted the end and had found it almost easier to live with no expectations except for death and pain rather than with a dubious and unlikely hope for rescue. Now that she had opened herself up to the possibility, the waiting for an answer was simply too much.

When Hilda confirmed that she had found the man and knew how to get to his secret location Erica was mad with joy.

"I'm afraid I have led you on, a little," Hilda put a downer on her boss's enthusiasm.

"What do you mean? Has he said that he won't see me? Let me meet him and negotiate. I am good at that, you know that."

"Well, I haven't been entirely honest with you," Hilda said sheepishly.

"Pardon me?"

"I've been economical with the truth and not told you everything that I should have. I so wanted you to give this a chance, that I kept a few things about Arpan from you. I sincerely hope they won't prove a stumbling point at this stage in the process."

"So…?"

"I gave you only certain newspaper articles and I even cut off the end of some of them, you may have noticed. There is more to his story than you know. He used to charge exorbitant fees."

"Yes! Of course! How could I have forgotten about that? That's what it was. I remember it now that was part of the drama about him in the press. I knew there was a reason why I disliked him so much."

"He asks for 50% of your wealth."

Erica breathed heavily.

"Right. How stupid of me to forget that. What an outrageous thing to do. Shameless exploitation of vulnerable people."

"So what do you think?" Hilda asked. "The statistics still speak for themselves. You'd be a fool if you didn't try."

"You're probably right," Erica admitted.

"We have one more problem," Hilda said.

"What would that be?" Erica asked. "After saying goodbye to my pension money, I'm curious what else you could throw at me."

When Hilda told her she had to sit down. "No way! That can't be right. What are the chances?"

"I know my dear," Hilda said with compassion in her voice. "I know. I've made enquiries and I think I have a solution for that, too."

It had been Hilda who had suggested the name change in the first place.

Erica stopped herself from indulging in those memories. They were not helping her, she would need to get more rest and make sure that tomorrow she'd be meeting Arpan again as Maria Miller and not let on anything about the fake name and their fateful connection whatsoever. She needed to get through this. Opening old wounds would only make her nervous and right now she had to put all that behind her. She caught a few more hours of sleep eventually before waking up, feeling dreadful, in pain and exhausted. Well, Arpan had warned her about that but he had also said it was a sign that the cancer was fighting back and therefore that the treatment was working.

Seriously missing her pain medication, she dismissed the idea of a morning stroll through the beautiful landscape around the B&B despite the warm and pleasant morning. This time of day had usually been filled with online surfing but without internet connection all she could do here was write in her diary about the experience so far. She had one of those unusual diaries that had a little ornamental locking mechanism. It was probably easy to break the lock open, so wasn't safe from being read by someone determined but at least Erica would always know if anyone had gained or tried to gain access to it. However, the lock would be at least enough of a deterrent for nosy people like the owner of the B&B and that gave her comfort.

At breakfast Mrs Jones was fortunately too busy with the other guests to pay much attention to Erica. Maybe she had realised that her nosiness wasn't welcome.

Instead, the woman was flirting with a group of what looked like gay couples on a hike. Erica smirked at the naiveté.

The fry up lay heavily in Erica's stomach and once again she worried that she might vomit, but eventually the feeling settled and she packed her things and made for the car.

Chapter 5

Arpan was practising his morning Qi Gong when she got to his place. The dog made a beeline for Erica as always, wagging his tail enthusiastically and jumping up on her to lick her face. She noticed how vibrant Arpan looked this morning - a far cry from the broken man she had encountered two days ago. His rebirth as Arpan from the ashes of Amesh seemed to have worked wonders for him.

His posture, his skin, everything about him seemed to radiate life. The way he stood and carried himself was like a different man entirely. Fortunately not in the manner of the arrogant man she remembered from the TV and magazine features on him. He seemed to have lost some of that unpleasantness and seemed calmer and levelled.

She stood in awe watching his every move as he did a martial art movement sequence: slow and in total control, seemingly effortless yet precise and exact like a ballet dancer. It was hard to tell if he had even noticed her coming out from behind the bushes or not, he should have heard her but he did not twitch or look towards her at all. After watching him for a good half hour she got over her fascination though and made her way towards the dome.

Inside Anuj was preparing the massage table and the syringe, her next dose of the blue-green coloured liquid.

"He's pretty focused today," she said as a way of opening the conversation.

"Yes, he's great. He's been doing this for almost two hours. He's collecting all the chi he can gather."

"I see," Erica replied unsure what to make of this last comment.

"You know it takes a lot out of him to do this. He pays for the treatment with his own chi," Anuj said, almost accusatively.

"You mean his energy?" she asked to make sure she understood correctly. Anuj nodded.

"He looks pretty vibrant to me right now," Erica protested. "In fact, I was just thinking to myself how much stronger he looks compared to two days ago, when, according to his words, he hadn't done any healing at all for ages. I could have sworn he was getting stronger through the act of healing, not the other way round."

"Trust me, that's not the case," Anuj said cryptically.

"I do trust you. You can't blame me for perceiving it this way though as I've been feeling like shit, excuse my French: absolutely drained. If it were not for all the references he has got, I would have started to doubt him and accused him of sucking the energy out of me, like a vampire."

"Trust me, you're getting the better deal here," Anuj said ominously. "By far!"

"What, do you think he won't take my money?" Erica joked sarcastically. "It's a pretty good deal for him, too. You've seen how much I am worth, and he's spending a week of his time, at the most."

"You still have a lot to learn, and have a long way ahead of you," Anuj said, shaking his head more to himself than to her. "Right now it sounds as if the cancer is doing the talking for you. You're quite venomous. Let's hope we get to the real you soon… Maria!" he added suspiciously slowly. Erica got a shot of adrenalin through her body, like a child who was caught with her hands in the cookie jar.

"I guess, so," she said quickly. "You're right, though. I should appreciate what he's doing for me, and of course I do. I know he hasn't done much healing of late and I am very grateful that he has made an exception for me. I had a rough night and don't know what I'm feeling or thinking other than exhaustion."

"It will get better," Anuj reassured her. "I heard it's always tough at the beginning. Like with most things in life, once you get accustomed to something it will change."

"He does look good, though," Erica repeated with a smile.

"It's all the energy he's collecting this morning through his Qi Gong," Anuj explained. "It's a slow and difficult process. He is doing this for you and as I said, it will cost him dearly."

"In what sense?" she asked.

"Energy wise. You should have seen him last night. He was really tired and worn out. I guess you will know more when you have finished the treatment course. By then, you'll understand the whole concept of healing and energy exchange much better."

"Don't you think that maybe the reason for his happiness is that he enjoys being Arpan again?" Erica wondered. "You know, to show what he can do to the world and to himself? Is there such a thing as complete altruism? Don't we all do good things to feel good about ourselves?"

"Then I guess you don't know Arpan at all and don't get what he's about," Anuj said. "Anyway, he will be finished soon and then will want to get started, so you had better get yourself on the table and ready."

"Fine," she said and complied.

"I'm afraid I will have to strap you to the table again. It's for your own protection, so that you won't convulse too much and fall off and hurt yourself. He said that at this stage of the treatment, some of his clients used to get strong trembling sensations, I hope you won't mind."

"Go ahead. It's probably a good thing. It was so bad last time that if I had been able to, I would have run off half way through. Besides, if you wanted to kill me, you would have done so already," she added jokingly.

At that moment, Arpan came in, positively radiating. Erica could almost feel the force of his energy before he even came close to her.

He didn't say a word but nodded towards Anuj, who took Erica's arm and injected the elixir. The burning sensation through her veins was worse than yesterday. Before she could say anything Arpan put his hands on her head and held it in a tight grip. Immediately her mind seemed to leave her body and raced up into the sky before floating thoughtlessly somewhere in the air. It was as if she wasn't even connected to her own body, although she wasn't looking down on herself like other people had reported from experiences they had had during operations and in life and death moments. Erica had always had reservations against such phenomena. What she was experiencing right now was more like a drug high, she reckoned, a sedative of the strongest kind.

Occasionally she thought she heard his voice; he was not speaking in English, more like gibberish, Aramaic perhaps or maybe even Hindu. The rhythmic and repetitive sound lulled her further into a trance-like state with no further sensory uptake from her body or the area surrounding her; a hypnotic spell that should have her worried but in this state, she couldn't care about anything. Then she fell asleep.

When she came to she was soaking wet with sweat and anything but pain-free.

"Oh my God," she sighed. "I was feeling so good and now it's all gone to pot again. How can I be so pain-free one minute and then the next so terrible? This is like torture," she complained.

"I'm sorry," Arpan said. "Believe me, it will be worth it. I took your mind out of your body so you wouldn't feel uncomfortable; sadly I can only do that while the treatment is in progress. The after effects are always a little trickier."

"You can say that again," she said. Anuj threw her that disparaging look that he had quickly perfected, probably with the intention to scold her for being ungrateful, and maybe he was right.

"Your cancer doesn't want to go," Arpan informed her. "But the battle we fought was a good one. If ever there is little or no pain at all after a treatment, that's when you need to start worrying. Cancer eats you alive, well it doesn't mean to, it just does. It isn't any more of a killer than humans are when it comes to the animals they eat. The cancer needs to survive and needs you to do it and to grow. That is his natural behaviour and it will hurt and kill you without meaning to. It's more or less predictable in that way; unless it feels threatened in its existence, either by the chemicals or from people like me. When it gets angry it behaves out of character and fights with everything it can and that is why you're experiencing such unusual and odd sensations that you normally wouldn't have to, even with something as nasty as pancreatic cancer."

"I'm sorry, Arpan," Erica said, "but this is bullshit. Cancer is cells dividing and dividing again, and growing. It doesn't have the intelligence or the power to make me sick by growing spontaneously in a calculated way or causing me to feel nauseous or anything like that. This doesn't make sense."

"Does what I do make sense to you?" he asked and looked at her with an almost mad and daring stare.

She shook her head.

"What do you mean when you say sense, anyway?" he continued. "There is more to our existence than the few things that can be measured. There is more than what makes sense in a conventional way. To me, after a lifetime of energy work and

46

learning, the things you cannot measure only gradually begin to make sense. I suppose it may take you a while longer just to open your horizons and open your mind a little."

"You have a point there," Erica conceded. She suddenly doubled over and almost retched. "Oh boy, I feel bad," she added. "Ow."

"Here, have some water," Anuj said and handed her a cup of water.

"Oh, that tastes rank," Erica said and almost spit it out. "What is this, rain water?"

Anuj just rolled his eyes and left the dome.

"Go outside," Arpan suggested. "Fresh air will do you good."

She was wobbly on her feet but managed to drag herself from the table to the clearing in front of the dome and towards Anuj, who had sat down in a meditation pose under a tree.

"Do you feel better now?" he asked her reluctantly, as if she had invaded his personal space.

"Not yet," she replied and gingerly sat down on a tree stump nearby. "I'm beginning to wonder if I will survive this treatment. It makes the chemo almost gentle in comparison."

"We would have to take your word for it," Anuj said, sounding disinterested and cold.

"How do you know Arpan, anyway?" she said, trying to break the ice and giving him a fragile smile.

"My mother used to work for him," he replied and took a deep breath, held it for ages and then exhaled. "About four years ago I... lost my way, shall we say. My mother tracked him down and asked him to take me in and sort me out as a special favour to her. He agreed and within a short space of time he turned my life around. I've never left."

"You must have plans to do something with your life, though. Get some education and get a job?" Erica said perplexed. "Do you envisage yourself living here for the rest of your life?"

"Of course I do. Maria, there's a lot about my life and Arpan that you don't understand. Sometimes I think that I'm only starting to get it myself: the beauty of it, the simplicity and so much more. I wish I could describe it. You need to feel it, experience it and live it. I learn more from this man than any university will ever teach me."

"You may not be able to make a living from what you're learning here. Right now he may be providing for you, but what if something happened to him? He is old, Anuj," Erica said with a warning tone.

"I will be provided for," Anuj said with a superior smile. "I won't lack anything whatsoever!"

"Of course," she said with a hint of sarcasm. "My money and that of all the others, I keep forgetting about that. Everything here looks so modest and unmaterialistic. It's easy to blank out the idea of the fortune he must have accumulated over the years, somewhere in an offshore account. You'll be inheriting his wealth and will be swimming in money. He must have millions," Erica said, somewhat disgruntled.

"No. You're wrong there," Anuj countered. "I said: I will be provided for. You are drawing your own conclusions. I never mentioned money and you know nothing if you're thinking along those lines. Nothing at all!" He seemed very angry all of a sudden.

"I hope you know what you're doing," Erica said, a bit more carefully. "You're still young and you will need to decide if you can live a life like this forever. You need to set yourself up first, establish your trade and skills, have some backup in case this 'business' goes under."

"Thank God this is no *business* then," Anuj replied. "What I learn from Arpan in life skills and outlook is more than I will ever need, Maria. With a foundation like that I'll be fine, whichever path I take in the future."

"That's easy to claim with all the cash," Erica snapped.

"I'm not planning to leave with any money from him," Anuj said abruptly. "He's provided me with enough already. Plenty."

He left his pose and stood up, ready to leave her alone.

"So you're saying that you'd be happy if you had to return to civilisation, penniless and stuck on a minimum wage job for the rest of your life?" she said in disbelief.

"Absolutely, yes," he replied calmly. "If your cancer has taught you nothing about the value of life and the great gift that it is, then you're nowhere near as clever as I thought. With the right attitude any existence can be bliss. What Arpan does is make me see the wonders, the gift of being alive every day and the happiness and serenity that comes from within. With those skills, the life that you described will be perfectly fine for me. Imagine how many people all over the globe would happily trade their lot for such a life. You of all people should know how little material things matter in the face of bare survival."

"You know how to argue your case," Erica admitted. "It would be more convincing if you didn't work for someone who takes as exuberant fees as Arpan does."

"Don't you see how your mind still circles around money? Well, his fees are in fact nothing more but a backhanded gift to yourself: it sets you free. The value you put on your life by paying him is an important part of raising your awareness and sorting out the priorities in your life. Arpan doesn't want or use the money for himself but he needs to take it from you in order for you to heal. The man hurts to take it."

"Explain that to my bank manager," Erica snapped again, but she realised that she had to change her attitude, at least on the surface, as not to offend the people that were trying to help her. She moved towards him and threw him another shy smile.

"I'm sorry," she added quickly. "Forget I said anything. I don't know what's wrong with me today. I signed the papers and I don't care about anything other than getting better. I know very well how unimportant money is in the face of death. The pain is getting to me and it makes me bitter and nasty."

"That's understandable. You have a lot of poison that needs to come out of your system. I can feel it too, your years of loneliness, of drinking and of misery."

She didn't like his current attitude.

"How would you know?" she challenged him.

"I've got eyes, and I can sense things, too," he replied.

"How many times have you seen him do this then?" Erica asked.

"This is the first time I've seen him do this," he admitted, "but he has taught me a lot."

"How did you know how to do the injection, then?" she asked confused. "You did it like a pro!"

"I had practice of that in a previous life," Anuj said with a broad grin. "Stop analysing everything," he added.

"So you are saying Arpan hasn't healed anyone during the entire time you've been with him?"

"He has healed me, the dog, himself and he gives to the Earth every day. I wish I could explain it better than this but as I said, at the end of your treatment course you might understand it a little more."

"What was wrong with you that needed healing, if I may ask?"

"I will tell you that another time," he said suddenly quite firmly. "I almost forgot. Arpan said for you to go home quickly. As you experienced such violent side effects yesterday, he thinks it is important for you to get home as soon as you are stable on your feet. You seem to have recovered enough to make a move. You don't want to get sick while driving."

"That's very reassuring," she said sarcastically.

"It's impossible to predict what will happen and how you will respond. Arpan said that sometimes the first bout of resistance is all that a specific cancer has to offer in terms of fight. Try not to expect anything, just go home and wait and see. Will you need me to come down to your car with you?"

"No, I'll be fine," Erica said stubbornly. "Thanks. Where is Arpan, by the way? Can I say goodbye to him and thank him before I go?"

"Arpan had to go lie down. The treatment has taken it out of him. Yesterday he slept for hours after your treatment."

"How odd. I read that he used to heal four to five people in a day," Erica said.

"He's older now and he's also taking this healing very seriously; like a comeback or a return to his old form. Before you arrived, I had only experienced the work he did with me. There were no injections, no straps and I had no violent reactions whatsoever. He was much gentler, although the effect was truly mind-blowing and amazing... I'm getting carried away again," he suddenly stopped himself. "Off you go. We'll see you tomorrow."

50

Chapter 6

Erica drove like the devil to get back to the B&B before another violent reaction could occur. She managed to dodge the nosy owner again and sat on her bed, waiting for her body to react. Nothing happened though, and after an hour she began to worry that the treatment wasn't working.

In her anxiety she decided to call Hilda for some distraction.

"Don't worry about it," her assistant reassured her after she heard the full report of the treatment and its after effects. "He knows what he's doing. Don't question everything and over-analyse. Have some faith."

"That's easier said than done," Erica admitted.

"I told you he's good, didn't I?" her former assistant asked but didn't wait for a reply. "You felt his strength, what else could you want as proof? I'm so glad he agreed to make an exception for you. You should feel honoured. Are you sure he hasn't figured out who you are?"

"His assistant once said my false name with a suspicious emphasis, as if that was meant to tell me something, but that might be my paranoia."

"How is his assistant towards you?"

"Unfriendly but very benign. I think he has a good heart and wants to look out for Arpan."

"And his questioning of your name was a one off thing?" Hilda asked.

"Yes."

"Sounds like paranoia to me," Hilda concluded. "Remember: if they know and are still treating you, then you're safe anyway," she reasoned.

"Unless they mean to torture me," Erica said jokingly. "I never read about the amount of pain in any of the paper cuttings. It does make me wonder."

"Nonsense! He's not that kind of person," Hilda said. "He's neither vindictive nor nasty. You have to trust me on this one, and you have to trust him."

"He keeps saying that, too. If trust is that important, it makes me think that it is one big placebo effect," Erica said dismissively.

"A positive attitude helps with everything in life. Don't worry about it being just a placebo effect. If it worked for almost all of his former clients I would take it without complaining."

"He's a very powerful man, that Arpan. He seems to read me like a book, he seems to know everything. I wonder if I should come clean about who I am and be done with it.

"That might be a good idea," Hilda disagreed. "He is very spiritually evolved and seems above petty revenge or interpersonal conflicts."

"If you say it like that it makes me doubt him again. It was not a petty issue between him and I, but a pretty huge one. I doubt I would be able to let that slide if the roles were reversed."

"I think he's quite capable of forgiving. Maybe he knows but doesn't feel a need to let that influence him?" Hilda guessed.

"You're probably right."

"The money has gone," Hilda said suddenly. "I checked it this morning. He left you 12.03%, isn't that funny?"

"That is funny. Weird funny. How do you know it is exactly 12.03%? Did you calculate that figure yourself?"

"No, it said so on the statement. Where the name of his company should appear he wrote: 'Left you 12.03%. You'll need it!' How bizarre is that?"

"You can say that again," Erica said. "Hilda, I feel I know too little about the man. Can you be a darling and send me the other press cuttings and articles, the ones you never sent to me. I know you must have them."

"What do you mean?" Hilda asked flustered. "The ones about the money? Darling, you know about that now, so what'd be the point?"

"You persuaded me with great articles that praised Arpan and his work. You said there were parts missing and I remember how some of the articles at the time went to town with accusations about the money and his practice. Maybe there is more to know about him. I should like to read them."

"So you can indulge in more cynicism and doubt?" Hilda said with a dismissive laugh. "No, I don't think so. You should be listening to soft music and enjoying the beautiful Welsh

52

countryside. Try to calm your overactive mind for once and enjoy the break. I know that once you're healed you'll be going back to your life and to that company as if nothing ever happened. Enjoy the peaceful moments while you can."

"And what are you doing besides your work? Are you practising what you preach?" Erica asked.

"Fair point," Hilda chuckled. "Do you want me to come and see you over the weekend?"

"I'm not sure yet. He hasn't even said how many treatments it will take," Erica said. "I hope not too many. On one hand they are great experiences, on the other they are an ordeal. I kind of hope that I will be home by Friday."

"His average treatment was five sessions spaced out over the course of ten days. You should definitely still be there for the weekend."

"He hasn't taken days off with me," Erica pointed out. "I have to go back there every single day. I'm not sure if he counts the first treatment or not, but I could be at three sessions already."

"Oh, well. It makes sense for him to power through, since he's only doing work on one person instead of five. He might as well get it over and done with," Hilda said.

"No, it doesn't quite add up. His assistant says that Arpan totally exhausts himself with my treatments, that he sleeps for hours and needs plenty of energy work to prepare for each session. It doesn't seem that he's in a very good shape, so why is he doing this in such a rushed and intense way? I myself would appreciate a break, this isn't pleasant for me either," Erica said. "Don't get me wrong I'm desperate to get it over and done with, but it is taking its toll on my body; a day off would not go amiss."

"Your cancer is very advanced," Hilda said quietly. "That might have something to do with it. Whatever reason he has, you have to start trusting him. You're turning over every little issue in your mind looking for doubt and questioning him: try to relax instead."

"You're right," Erica said, "Thank you!"

"Get some rest," Hilda said. "I need to get back to work. Since you left the office is in complete chaos. Your temporary replacement is not getting anything quickly enough. I'm putting in a lot of extra hours to train her and to make up for her uselessness. Me, her assistant! We're all praying for you to come back. Even your arch enemy Helen has said she would trade your snippy comments and swearing over the incompetence that we are forced to deal with. You don't know what you've got until it is gone, apparently. So get better soon, for our sake!"

"Hilda, you're a darling, thank you!"

Erica hung up and stretched out on her bed. The conversation had cheered her up, but she felt odd that there was no sickness, nausea or pain today. If there was, she would feel a little more certain that Arpan had what it took. She laughed at the irrationality of her reasoning. Well, she suddenly noticed, there was some of her regular pain coming back - although nothing as violent as yesterday or the day before; nothing like the reaction that had come from the elixir on the first day and which was clearly not a symptom of her clinical condition. How could she ever be sure that Arpan's treatment was working? She missed the reliability of western medicine, its predictability and its reassuring empiric data and statistics.

The cancer could have spent all of its energy already, Arpan had more or less said as much, but there could also be even more violent reactions to come. Could, could and more could, but no will or won't. She hated that.

Just then her stomach doubled over in a tormenting cramp as if someone had punched her with an iron bar. Before she could think about it she threw up on the carpet. Dammit, she would have to ask the annoying landlady for a cloth and explain the situation. After all the avoiding she had done with that woman. There came another bout of vomit. She rushed to the toilet, in time to brave another wave of nausea followed by diarrhoea. As her body was putting her through this painful outburst however Erica sighed with huge relief. She needed this to restore her confidence and trust in Arpan. To her desperate mind, this meant that his elixir was working and that she would be cured, of that she became suddenly more certain. She eased gladly now into the inevitable and for the first time in her life 'enjoyed' being ill. There was something oddly therapeutic in her surrender, a rewarding sensation in becoming one with the disease and its effects. She embraced it with all her might. Whereas before she had tried to stop and fight it, she now felt as if she was merely hanging on to the rails of a fast moving roller coaster ride, but was now one with its motion and content with wherever it might take her.

Before long the storm in her body calmed down and she sank exhausted back on her bed. The room reeked of vomit and the last thought on her mind was to get up and wipe it up but she sank into a deep sleep and didn't wake until midnight again. The alarm clock said 12.03. She laughed at the coincidence. As far as being ill was concerned, it seemed as if there was a pattern emerging and she was none too pleased about it. She was starving but had no appetite either. She moped up the sick and sprayed her perfume on it. It didn't vastly improve the situation but it took the edge of it. Thank God that Arpan had left her that little money, which she would need to have the carpet cleaned.

12.03%. What a joker.

Erica forced some cereal bars down her throat. She had to eat something or she thought that she really would die. Compared to those acupuncture and Reiki sessions this treatment was unbelievably violent, a real physical fight for survival and she wondered how Arpan had got away with it all those years ago, especially when he first began his technique. This was such a torturous procedure, how had he managed to get his first patient to agree to have this done to them? If Erica had not read the newspaper articles with the assurance of hundreds of success stories, she would not have been sure that this was leading anywhere and probably would not continue with it, regardless of her desperation. Who had been his patient zero, the first guinea pig? She would have to ask Arpan about that tomorrow. It could not have been easy to establish himself as healer with such a great reputation when he had to subject his guinea pigs to so much pain first. Who would have agreed to such a violent treatment and so much pain when there was no proof of a healing? Well, come to think of it, maybe somebody very desperate. To make it from a local insider tip amongst hard-core new age hippies to a minor celebrity, who made waves even beyond the national level, had to have taken time and a lot of luck.

Erica knew a fair bit about the alternative scene but only what her eccentric Aunt Bethany had preached to her: Nostradamus, Astrology, Numerology, Madam Blavatsky and the 'Spirit Mediums' and of course all those famous magic healers. A true child of the sixties, Aunt Bethany had always been flamboyant and 'out there', which had made her more of a comical figure to her niece than a woman of knowledge and power.

"Rasputin healed the haemophiliac Russian Royals," the often ridiculed woman always had used as her biggest argument. "How can you explain that? He made history with his abilities, but of course Stalin had to erase that from the documents, so that everyone would be equal. I tell you, some people have gifts beyond our wildest dreams," Bethany would say and reel off stories of miracle healers and their successful cases, but also about their slow path to fame and respect for their abilities. Even in Aunt Bethany's receptive circles it would have taken a long time before trust in a healer like Arpan was established, before word of mouth got out and went beyond the small local radius. Eventually it would reach a critical point after which the healer became established firmly enough for newspapers to investigate and for society to notice. Bethany of course had known hundreds of these people and had wasted her fortune letting these people do their magic on her, yet Erica didn't buy into it. The determination to convert everyone to her way of thinking had had something of a desperate cry for attention and had the opposite effect than what was intended.

It was no surprise that Erica never took to the Arpan phenomenon when it broke. By then Bethany had died of an AIDS related disease, something that none of the healers had been able to stop.

Erica's thoughts got distracted when she heard a violent knocking at her door.

"Are you in there?" the landlady called. "I can see the light. What is that smell?"

Erica sighed at the prospect of having to face the nosy woman but she had no choice as to deal with it right now.

"Good evening, Mrs Jones. I'm terribly sorry, I'm not feeling too well," she said as soon as she had opened the door. "I was sick," she added and pointed at the floor.

Like a whirlwind Mrs Jones walked into the room with the lightness of a 20 year old, despite her being closer to 60.

"I'll reimburse you for the damage," Erica said quickly to make sure she wouldn't get drawn into an argument or an angry sermon. She really wasn't in the mood for this.

"Oh love, don't you worry about that," the woman said reassuringly. "This carpet has seen worse over the years. I have a wonderful industrial carpet cleaner in the garage; I'll get my husband to get it out tomorrow morning. Are you alright, love? You look even worse than when you arrived. The country air doesn't seem to be doing its magic on you, I can tell. Are you ill or something?"

Erica looked to the floor, embarrassed. She wasn't used to such directness: in London people didn't ask or care. She was caught off guard and hadn't prepared an excuse to dodge these unexpected questions.

"I'd rather not talk about it," was all she could think to say.

Mrs Jones looked disapprovingly at her and stuck her hands onto her hips.

"I don't mean to intrude, if that's what you are implying, love, but I really should know if something major is wrong with you. We're out in the sticks her and if I find you unconscious or something then I need to know how serious it is, so I can call an ambulance or someone. Are you on any medication that I should know about?" and with that she looked around the desk and the bedside table as if it were entirely natural.

"Dear Mrs Jones, I'm sorry, but could we please discuss this in the morning? I'm awfully tired."

"Of course, but if you don't wake up or have some fit?" the landlady asked with a provocative dramatic tone. "I really need to know a little, don't I!"

"Fair enough," Erica said, too tired to think this through. "I have cancer. However, if I collapse it will be exhaustion. I don't mean any disrespect but I wanted a few days to myself in the middle of nowhere, to come to terms with it. Please don't intrude any further. I left London so I could be in peace. Thank you of course. I do appreciate your kind concern," she added quickly.

"Say no more, love," Mrs Jones said and awkwardly grabbed Erica's hand squeezed it strongly and left, all the time nodding her head quickly.

Erica closed the door and breathed a heavy sigh. So much about her plan for anonymity. Well, at least Erica wouldn't have to pay for the carpet. Now that she was on a tight budget for the foreseeable future, those things would now matter. Probably part of the lesson that Arpan wanted to teach her and the world.

She found herself unable to sleep so she began to write in her diary until eventually her head sank onto the table and she fell into a deep, dreamless sleep.

Chapter 7

"Wake up, darling," were the first words she heard the next morning. Mrs Jones was pulling at her shoulders. Erica looked up and slowly took in what was going on.

"What are you doing in my room?" she asked angrily.

"Don't get all upset, love. I had to make sure you were alright. I couldn't let you die here, could I?" Mrs Jones said, ignoring the anger and speaking as if there could be no doubt about her right to enter the room and take charge of Erica's day.

"Thank you, but I can take it from here," Erica said, stood up and straightened herself into a position of composure and dominance in front of her landlady. It helped that she was a little taller, she thought.

"Alright, keep calm! Now that I know you're well I can leave anyway." She cast a searching look around the room before turning round and heading towards the door.

"I take it you won't have breakfast either, today? You really should, you know. Your body needs strength."

"Thank you," Erica said. She would have liked to have some bacon this morning but now, that it came at the cost of conversation, she was happy to stick with her cereal bars. She had brought tons of them. Maybe, after the treatment today, if she was fit enough, she would drive to the nearest village and have a proper meal there. Somehow, though, she didn't think it likely."

"Fine, suit yourself," Mrs Jones replied, attempting a gracious smile. "When would be good for my husband to have a go at the soiled carpet, love?"

"I'll be leaving in half an hour at the latest," Erica reassured her worried landlady.

"Where could you possibly go in a state like this? Oh dear, well it's your decision of course. When will you be back?" Mrs Jones asked.

"I don't know that yet. I hope by lunchtime, but possibly later than that."

"You will need to let the carpet dry out a little, if we were to start the cleaning now you shouldn't come back in here until the evening. You are welcome to come into my lounge and sit there with me. I usually watch 'Countdown' and 'Deal or No

Deal' in the afternoon. Would be great to have some company, and I'm sure you could really do with some of that, too."

"Thank you for the offer and for the heads up," Erica said, moving towards Mrs Jones. She grabbed the door handle and closed in on her 'visitor' until the woman got the hint and moved out of the doorframe backwards into the hallway.

"See you later," Erica said and closed the door at last.

Phew! That had been an unpleasant way to start the day. Erica had a shower and put on clean clothes, then she packed all of her documents into her back pack. She wouldn't put it past Mrs Jones to have a good rummage through everything here while the room was empty. Erica couldn't afford that, not with the non-disclosure agreement she had signed.

Once she had groomed herself she couldn't get out of the door fast enough. Fortunately she managed to get into her car without bumping into the busybody again.

It was a beautiful morning, she noticed. The clouds had all disappeared and a blue sky allowed a youthful sun to burn of the morning mist and to warm up Erica's skin through her clothes. Despite her anger over the annoying landlady, her mood began to improve. She noticed how she had not even once thought about taking pain killers. The pain and discomfort were still blatantly prominent but, like yesterday during the treatment, she began to ease into the disease with some kind of resignation, surrender or acceptance; however, which of the three she was not entirely sure of.

Arpan and Anuj were performing one of their martial art morning rituals together in the clearing. Deeply focused in their interplay they didn't seem to notice her. The dog Ashank came up to greet Erica as usual but then he lay down by the side of the clearing and rested. Erica sat down next to him on the tree stump and watched in awe as the two men moved in synchronicity and perfect grace. It was quite a beautiful spectacle. They did not stop to acknowledge her, for all she knew they might really not have even seen her come in, so focused and absentminded did they appear.

When they finally finished Erica clapped her hands in applause.

"Beautiful," she said appreciatively. "Just beautiful!"

"It is," Arpan replied. "Not that that should be important."

"True," Erica admitted. "I guess you're collecting energy again for today's healing?"

He smiled and shook his head playfully.

"Not this morning, no. We have a different day ahead of us today," he said rather ominously.

"I'm glad to hear it," Erica said relieved. A day without the intensity of the last few sessions was something to look forward to. "I heard that you used to leave more time between treatments. I wondered what was wrong with me that you needed to do them on consecutive days, even though Anuj said the healing is such a strain on you."

Arpan frowned.

"I'm sorry," she said quickly, panicking that she had overstepped a mark. "I meant to say how much I appreciate you putting in so much energy. It must be a relief for you to have day off."

"I'm still treating you today," he corrected her firmly. "I'm merely preparing for it in a different way. You don't need to occupy your mind with any of this. Don't listen to Anuj. Ease into the day. I'll be taking care of everything for you."

"I see," she said, but she did not.

Arpan suddenly became more business-like and said:

"You do have an aggressive type of cancer, I'm sure you've already sensed that from the violent reactions. I have always treated the harder cases on consecutive days if I could. I doubt that the papers you've read ever got into that much detail about me. Anyway, today we need to tackle our enemy with a different force, to confuse it and lull it into a false sense of security. That, too, is part of my regular routine," he explained.

"So no elixir and being strapped to the table today?" Erica asked excitedly.

"I'm afraid I will need to administer the elixir later, but first we're going to do a few other things," he said. "Come with me!"

He jumped up and ran into the woods behind the dome.

Erica took a few seconds to react but then she feared she might lose him, since he was running so quickly, and she tried to catch up with him. She realised that her recent breathlessness had gone. Had she only imagined the water in her lungs, she wondered. She could actually breathe deeply for the first time in days.

"Where are you?" she called out, "I can't see you, Arpan."

"Find me!" Arpan called from a distance but she couldn't make out from which direction.

She kept running towards where she thought she had heard him only then to hear him from a different location. She could not believe how much land Arpan owed. She had always assumed that there would be a fence behind the house to make the grounds obvious but there seemed to be no fence or barrier anywhere.

"Find me!" she heard again, this time from a different direction. She turned and ran where she thought the voice had come from. Was it still Arpan, or was that Anuj now? What kind of silly games were they playing? Again.

"Find me!" from the opposite direction. She ran one way, turned and ran again, until quite suddenly she had to stop and spontaneously burst into a fit of hysterical laughter. She sat down on the wet moss floor and let it all happen.

"Find me... find me!" she heard again and again.

"Oh, find me yourself," she replied, giggling. "I'm not moving."

Then there was silence. She waited for a few minutes, surprised at the sudden end to the game. After 15 minutes or so she started to feel unease.

"Where are you?" she called out, but there was no reply. She got up and tried to figure out where she was in relation to the dome. The terrain was uneven against the hill, so it should have been easy to find her bearings but she had run trusting the voices without taking note of landmarks. The trees were quite thick in some places and she found it hard to figure out where she should be headed.

It couldn't be that she had got lost on someone's small piece of land, she thought, but she really couldn't make out where she was.

"Where are you?" she called out to no reply. A deep sense of abandonment settled over her all of a sudden. "I can't find you, Arpan. Help me, this isn't funny anymore."

When there still was no answer she felt a deep existential fear and angst that cut through her like a knife. Feelings from her long gone past flooded through her and what she thought she had put to rest suddenly felt fresh and hurtful. There was a sense of hopelessness that she had run from all of her life and it had found her here and took hold of her being. Her heart sank and she sat down in resignation, feeling she was about to burst into tears or give up on life altogether.

"Good job," Arpan suddenly said, standing directly behind her. "That should have brought some life into you," he added and then he put his hands on her shoulders and she once more felt the enormous heat and warm energy radiating from them.

"Why did you do this?" she asked.

"Shhh…," he said and as she went limp he lowered her gently to the ground. She was overwhelmed by her feelings. Happiness had been rapidly followed by fear and now relief, but also confusion and doubt. What was he doing to her, those were her last thoughts before rational reason disappeared from her mind. She felt the prick of a needle and the familiar burning sensation in her veins, then she passed out and remembered nothing.

When she came to, she was still lying on mossy ground, surrounded by blankets and cushions. She could see the back of the dome.

Anuj was sitting behind her, reading a book by Osho.

"Why did you do that to me?" she asked. "That was really scary, I had no idea the grounds were so extensive. I thought I was lost."

"Maybe they appeared to you as if they were extensive," Anuj explained. "You really couldn't get lost here, but Arpan can make you feel as if you were."

"Nonsense," she refused to agree. "He may be good at reading people, but he can't influence what I think with his mind. He had neither touched me nor injected me with anything before I ran after him into the woods."

Anuj just shrugged his shoulders.

"At the end of the day, what matters is that you had those feelings. Arpan explained it to me yesterday evening. You must have heard of primal scream therapy?"

She nodded, a little reluctantly and apprehensively.

"Well, it is something like that. You really needed to let out your inner child. You still run around like you are an executive with your list of tasks to attend to and the minutes of inconsequential meetings to write up. You needed to come off that treadmill, and it worked a treat. Once you were playful and vulnerable, he let you get lost, to confront your primal fears. It turns out that abandonment is one of them, but not the most important one."

"That's utter tosh," she said laughing confidently. "I'm one of the most independent people you'll ever meet."

"I'm sure that's what you think but from where I'm standing it looks quite different. Not that it matters anyway. The point is that we needed the elixir to hit you at your most vulnerable. It is that core of your being that the cancer can feed off because you don't acknowledge and nurture it yourself. We got you there and it was on that ground that we met the cancer today. Look at yourself; you're still in a foetal position."

He was right! She never slept in that position. Past boyfriends had complained about her spreading herself out like a starfish when she slept, pushing them to the edge of the bed, many falling off during the night.

"We all have a vulnerable child inside of us that needs to be nurtured and you, like everyone else, have forgotten how to look after it. This was the most amazing transformation I have ever seen," Anuj said.

"I thought you had said that you never saw Arpan heal anyone," she said confused.

"Before I came here I've been around the healer's circuit, Mother took me everywhere she could think of to make me better."

"What exactly was wrong with you?" Erica asked. "You never told me," she added, accusingly.

"I'm not going to tell you today," he said gently. "We're talking about you and your health not about my history."

"I want to know about you and Arpan, so I can try to understand what's going down here," she said.

"That's the business woman in you talking again, trying to rationalise things and demanding answers but that won't help you at all."

"You can't seriously expect me to behave like a little child, be treated like a school girl and do as I'm told, like your dog here!" she exclaimed with outrage.

"Take it or leave it," Anuj said. "Trust, and have faith!"

He pulled himself up, closed his book and shook the dirt off his trousers.

"I will tell Arpan that you have come round. Stay where you are and give yourself more time before getting up. You're still under the influence," he said and winked at her cheekily.

Feeling rebellious she tried to get up, but felt a strong wave of dizziness and sank back down on the ground.

"I told you," he said with a smirk and left her alone.

She didn't like being left on her own but didn't want to admit it. God, she was behaving childishly, she realised; it was utterly humiliating. She stayed on the ground for another half hour or so, then she felt the urge to get back to civilisation. She picked up the pillows and the blanket and carried them towards the dome.

"Put them by the door," Anuj told her when she entered the clearing from behind the dome. He was reading his Osho book on the tree stump, with Ashank lying by his feet, and only briefly looked up.

"Is that it?" she asked. "Shall I see myself out?"

"Yes, please. Arpan has gone to lie down again."

"Is he going to be alright?" Erica asked suddenly. "You mentioned the price he has to pay for the treatment several times. I hope I'm not surviving at his expense."

"It's a little late to worry about that now," Anuj said. "He made the decision and he's taking the risks he wants to take. You needn't worry about it. He wants to see you again tomorrow morning."

"Will I be able to go to the village for some dinner, or am I going to be too weak for that, too?" she asked.

"I'd rather you didn't go," Anuj said. "If you do get ill while you're in a public place then you'll have to do an awful lot of explaining to do. Arpan really appreciates his anonymity here. We don't want to risk that by you telling anyone inadvertently what we're doing here."

"I probably should tell you something then," she said with seriousness. "I was sick on the carpet in my B&B last night. I told the owner that I have cancer. I was certain that would keep her out of my hair, but she's been on my case ever since. She came into my room this morning and woke me up. The door was locked, so she must have used her own key. I was just thinking earlier, that if she did this this morning, she might do this again and may even have already done so before. My privacy there is certainly compromised."

"In that case try to go out in public as little as possible. Don't tell the woman where you're going and what you're doing here. Make something up. There's a holistic health centre not far from here. You could always pretend that you're taking some courses over there. The locals hate the place, so it won't invite many questions."

"What if they see my car parked at the bottom of the hill?"

"Say you went for a walk around here. If you continue on that path past our gate you can reach a wonderful plateau with a little lake. It's a steep walk, mind, so you'll have to complain about that to be convincing."

"There are days when I just cannot place you here in this spiritual life," Erica said. "You can be so worldly and street wise."

"That's probably why I'm here," Anuj said with a wink. "Someone has to look after Arpan."

"Was it heroin you did?" she asked. "Must have been, the way you're with the needles. You said you had prior experience."

She was expecting him to pull away and get angry at the accusation, but instead he just smiled and touched her shoulder gently, as if to console her.

"I wish that had been the case," he said cryptically. "I can see that you won't let this go until you find out. I might as well tell you then, if it keeps your need for human contact satisfied and prevents you from talking to the villagers. It's not an interesting story, I have to warn you."

"I will be the judge of that," she said, and sat down next to him. Ashank, the dog, licked her hands and then settled down comfortably by her feet on the floor.

"The thing about me and needles has a simple explanation. My younger brother was diabetic and needed regular injections. I learned how to do it, so I could relieve my mother sometimes."

"You would have preferred being addicted to heroin to that?" she asked outraged. "How can you say that?"

"Of course," he replied. "Getting over heroin is hard but quite doable. My brother's diabetes was a tough daily struggle that was never going to end."

"You said was," she observed. "Was he healed?"

66

"No, he got hit by a car in a stupid accident," Anuj said, appearing very strong and stable for someone revisiting such a dark part of his past, she thought. "I lost the plot a little after that. I was only 16 and took to it very badly."

"What did you do?"

"I did nothing. I stayed indoors, slept and stopped communicating. If I had done drugs or alcohol, they could have put me in rehab. I was clean but I was broken all the same, and they found no handle to it."

"What about counselling and medication?" Erica asked. "That should have bridged you over the worst."

"You'd think that, but I refused that solution and so did my mother. She is very alternative therapy minded and was never going to have me either institutionalised or pumped full of drugs. So we had hypnotherapists, healers, sacro-cranial therapists, dowsers, tarot card readers, intuitive healers, spiritual healers and many more through our door, but I responded to nothing."

"None of them could help you, but Arpan could?" Erica said.

"Seems so," he said. "We were all surprised to find this out ourselves, most of all Arpan, or Amesh as he was already called then. I hardly noticed anything going on around me at the time, I was lethargic, submerged in nihilism and darkness. I hated my life, I hated the universe for taking Tom like that, I blamed myself for not taking good enough care of him and I blamed my mother for the same reason. I hated all those people who came and wouldn't leave me alone, when it was obvious that they had nothing to offer that would help me."

"Did you even try and give them a chance?" she asked.

"Well, nobody could bring Tom back, could they," Anuj said with a grin. "Then Amesh came, and he simply put his hands on my shoulders. He said nothing, asked nothing of me and suddenly it all became loose inside of me. At least I could cry and let out some of my hurt. The way he looked at me was odd: he was as perplexed as I was over the fact that this was working. My mother had brought so many people into our home who came and went without having any impact on me, we didn't think for one second that Amesh would really be any different. He offered for me to come and stay with him here, and the prospect of being somewhere remote, away from everyone, was too good an opportunity to miss. And so you know now that I have had plenty of experience with healing over the years, and why I'm so good with needles."

"Does your mother ever come and visit?"

"Rarely, you see, she and Arpan had a big fall out when she was working for him. She contacted him out of sheer desperation, she never thought he would actually show. Despite everything that has happened since, they still find it very difficult to be around each other. They never told me what happened between them but it must have been bad."

"So much secrecy and mystery," Erica said. "I would have thought it would be different in such esoteric, new age circles."

"Humans will always be humans," he said, laughing.

"Why don't you come with me to the village? That way I could go for some good food and avoid making a scene or being questioned if I get sick."

"We don't interact with the people here," he told her. "If we need something we drive all the way to the nearest city, where nobody recognises us. It's a tough job to keep your anonymity, as you have noticed. It's best not to be noticed at all. You're too weak for all of this anyway. You can stay here for dinner if you're that desperate for company. I guess Arpan won't mind."

"No, I don't want to impose," Erica said. "Thank you. Maybe another day."

"Suit yourself," he replied. "You might want to take a few minutes deciding what you want from your life, though, when you get it back after this. You seem awfully confused. One minute you want to go to the village for food and company and when I offer you the same thing here, you simply back off again. If you deny yourself all the time, you'll never be happy. You are awfully complicated."

"You're right. I am."

Chapter 8

Taking Anuj's advice, Erica decided against going to the village and opted for the unpleasant but safer prospect of returning to the B&B. The carpet in her room had already been cleaned, the smell of the cleaning detergent was present the second she entered the house. Mrs Jones had left a huge note with a warning on the room door but Erica went in regardless and sat down on her bed. She thought she had dodged the landlady but within seconds the nosy woman knocked on the door and simply entered the room.

"Please don't come into the room uninvited," Erica said politely but with an edge of outrage and surprise.

"Love, I told you not to stay in the room until the carpet is clean, you can't have missed the sign. I need to check how it dries up. Get up and come to the lounge," Mrs Jones said with her forceful and dominant manner and she walked up to Erica and grabbed her by the wrist. Erica pulled her arm away and looked at the intruder with wide, angry eyes.

"Please don't touch me, Mrs Jones. I'm very sorry but I hurt and I'm tired and the last thing I want to do is see or speak with anyone," she said and shifted her body towards the other end of the bed, away from the bossy woman.

"Can't have that, I'm afraid," Mrs Jones insisted. "We need to think of the carpet. Get your things and come with me."

"Do you have another room available? I could rent another room for the day," Erica suggested, starting to feel nauseous again. This timing was bad.

"You already caused us a lot of extra work. I'm not going through the palaver of cleaning a separate room because you refuse to cooperate. We're full up anyway. Now get over yourself and come with me."

Erica wanted to pack her things and leave but her sixth sense issued some warnings which made it clear that that was not a viable option. Furthermore, her stomach felt unstable to say the least and she just didn't have enough energy to argue.

She gave in and followed Mrs Jones to the family lounge where the TV was reeling off one mid-afternoon quiz show after another. Fortunately Erica was left alone for most of the afternoon, so she sat in the corner writing in her diary, making sure that she was unseen while doing so. Mrs Jones fortunately seemed, when in the room, transfixed by the quiz shows and tried to answer the questions passionately. Every so often she had to leave the room to keep herself busy with the other guests and doing chores in the kitchen, but she still kept popping in with tea and biscuits, a blanket, a hot water bottle and a bucket 'for emergencies'. Her interest had surprisingly shifted away from Erica, which was reassuring. Meanwhile, Erica was experiencing only mild cramps and sweating.

"I made you some dinner," Mrs Jones said around 6pm. "Here are some bangers and mash, you need something solid to line your stomach."

Before Erica could even respond the woman disappeared. Greedily Erica started in on her meal, only now realizing how hungry she is.

"I think it's okay for you to go back to your room now," Mrs Jones announced half an hour later and Erica didn't need a second invitation to do so.

The smell of the detergent had permeated everything in the room and made her feel nauseous - very dangerous after she had eaten such a huge meal that weighed heavily on her stomach. When she emptied her bag to continue writing in her diary about the day she'd had, she noticed that the documents were in a different order. She couldn't be entirely sure, but she had a habit of putting the hardback diary at the back of her bag and now it was at the front. Erica was too drained to be completely certain, but she could have sworn someone had rummaged through her bag. It did not bode well. She rushed towards the door and locked it, then had a closer look. Sadly, the bangers and mash were coming back up and Erica was busy in the bathroom for the next hour or so and when her body finally calmed down again, she had forgotten all about it.

She woke once again at midnight – 12.03 - fully clothed and soaked in sweat. She took a shower and then went back to bed, feeling much better. She texted Hilda, to see if the woman could send her a few Osho books for Anuj but then she reconsidered. Hilda had done enough for her and Anuj probably didn't need or want anything from her either.

The thought of someone having gone through her bag was disturbing. Maybe it would be better if she left the B&B and took up residence somewhere else. There was something eerie about the landlady and she found her somewhat untrustworthy, or was that simply paranoia? However, the bag had been unsupervised while she was at Arpan's and it could have been one of the two men who had looked through it, which was more likely. Had they found something in there that would blow her cover as Maria Miller? She examined everything closely for anything in there that could give her away as Erica, but she didn't see anything. Relieved she fell back to sleep.

At seven am Mrs Jones knocked on her door and rattled at the lock.

"Are you alright in there?" Mrs Jones shouted through the door. "I told you not to lock the door, love. You are ill, we need to make sure you're alright. Will you be having breakfast this morning?"

"Leave me alone," Erica shouted angrily. "I'm still asleep."

"Is all I needed to know," the woman called from the other side of the door. "Just checking you are alive and well. Breakfast is being served shortly, so get on with it and join the other guests when you're ready. You mustn't again leave without eating.

Erica got dressed, took her bag with everything personal in it and made for the lounge. She might as well eat before heading out; the woman was right. She would have to find other ways to keep the woman at arm's length and maybe being friendly towards her would be more successful.

"You behave like someone who has a lot to hide," Mrs Jones said as she served eggs, bacon and toast. "If I didn't know any better I'd say you're a spy," she added and giggled hysterically at her own joke.

Erica looked at her food and said nothing in reply.

"I was only joking, like," Mrs Jones said hastily but then she added with a twinkle in her eye: "Where are you heading today, may I ask?"

Erica pointed at her full mouth and chewed extra slowly. The landlady let out a deep sigh, shook her head at the secrecy and eventually left the room asking no further questions. At the earliest opportunity Erica left the B&B by the backdoor, rushed to her car and took off.

Anuj was quite alarmed when he heard about Mrs Jones and her intrusive nature.

"At least I have a lock on my diary," Erica said. "Because my work is quite competitive I've always done that. She could only have seen the newspaper cuttings."

"In that case there is not much harm done," Anuj said. "It's not ideal that she knows your interest in Arpan but if you can throw her off course by saying something about being a journalist or writer, she might lose interest. You can leave all that stuff here with us from now on," he suggested.

"Maybe I should go and stay somewhere else?" she suggested.

"No, I think it's better to stick with the devil you know. It's an easier environment to control now that we understand the place and the woman a little better. There is only the one person to watch out for and to keep out of your business. In the village we wouldn't know who else might be interested in you. There could even be horny men pursuing you."

"In my current state I very much doubt that," Erica said with a brave smile.

He shook his head: "I'd say, stay with what you know."

She was a little suspicious that he took the incident so lightly, which fuelled her worries and mentally she added him to the list of possible people who may have gone through her stuff. Until she knew who her friends and enemies really were, leaving it here was not a safer option. Did Anuj have a hidden agenda? He was definitely scarred by life and there was something dark and secretive about him, even after he had opened up and finally told her about his brother.

"Fine. So what am I going to experience today?" She asked with a playful tone of a long suffering customer.

"I actually don't know," he said matter of factly. "Arpan hasn't told me, yet."

"I notice he's not doing any exercises this morning."

"He did them earlier by moonlight," Anuj said. "Whenever there's a full moon, that's what he does. He gets up in the middle of the night and stares at it. You should do that sometime. It's very intense and exciting but it recharges your senses like nothing else does in the world. Of course, if you live in London, it won't have the same power – you can't see the moon properly there."

"I guess not in the same way. Everything here seems more intense. It's been years since I've been outside of London and I'm starting to get it."

Arpan suddenly came out of the dome, dressed in the same ceremonial, multi-coloured dress he had worn a few days ago. Erica was a little put off by the pompous impression this gave her and had to suppress a little giggle. Instead of greeting her he just looked at her intensely as he approached her, then he stood in front of her, took her face in his hands and kept very uncomfortable eye contact. He was obviously trying to communicate with her telepathically, but she didn't get what his message was meant to be. It was half frightening, half comical the way he stared until he suddenly got through to her and she felt an enormous strength emanating from his eyes. It was as if he was taking over her mind and she surrendered to his might. She must have moved without noticing as she suddenly felt there was a chair behind her and let herself sink onto it. Anuj tied her to the chair, put a blindfold over her eyes and injected the elixir.

Erica felt drowsy more than anything else and was worried that she might fall out of the chair but Arpan should know what he's doing and she thought: 'I need to trust.'

"This will hurt a little," Arpan finally broke the silence and then she felt his hands passing through her skin and reaching for her cancer cells. The sensation was surreal, not painful but extremely uncomfortable and intrusive. As he began with what felt like the pulling out of the cells from her body in small clusters, there was some pain after all. She was surprised at the number of places he pulled cells out of. She didn't even know the location of all her secondary cancers, as far as she knew she was riddled with them – 'too many to mention individually'. He seemed to know what he was doing. Only now she remembered in her blur how Hilda had mentioned that Arpan could sense cancer cells. But taking them out? She desperately tried to hold onto these thoughts but they just seemed to be disappearing from her mind.

She must have had fainted because the next thing she knew, she was lying on the floor, supported by pillows and blankets, on her side with a pool of vomit next to her.

"Congratulations," Anuj said. "That is the worst bit of the treatment behind you."

73

"No kidding," she said sarcastically. Her body was aching badly, all the places Arpan had touched inside of her gave the impression of bleeding and stung like fresh cuts.

"Was that psychic surgery?" she asked confused. "It hurt as if it were real."

She looked at Arpan for a reply but he had turned his back to her and didn't seem to have heard her.

"Arpan," she said. "Did it go well?"

The man looked up at the sky and stretched his hands up in the air in a dramatic gesture, seemingly in a trance himself.

"Why won't he talk to me?" Erica asked Anuj. "He hasn't spoken to me today at all."

"He will speak to you when he's ready."

As if on cue Arpan lowered his arms and his head and walked straight towards the dome and then disappeared behind it.

"I know that you want me to have blind faith in him for the sake of the treatment but I could really do with the occasional reassurance and communication," Erica protested. "You admitted that you don't know much about what he's doing to me, so it would be great to speak to him about it directly."

Disinterestedly Anuj responded: "I will tell him how you feel," and entered the dome.

Shortly after, Arpan came out, wearing worn out jeans and a woolly jumper: he reeked of petrol.

"The operation was a complete success," he said and gave her an encouraging smile.

"Psychic surgery?" she asked. "I never read anything about that in any of the articles about you."

"Well, I always asked all of my patients not to disclose the exact methods I'm using, and while some of them made it to the press all the same, others never did. This 'surgery' is a new method that I only developed last night. It came to me in a dream and I can see how this improves the entire routine I normally perform. I used to pull the cells out with some magnetic force, but using my hands is much more appropriate in my opinion. I guess my hands were not ready for it back then. I was told in my dream to cleanse myself and burn everything I touched afterwards, though. I came into real contact with the cancer cells this time. An odd sensation."

"How did you develop the original 'routine' as you call it, in the first place?" Erica asked, worried that Arpan had changed his already proven methods for a spontaneous fancy spur of the moment idea that did not have the same reliability.

"That also came to me in some of my dreams," Arpan said, "I spent years looking for it. Dr Usui, the founder of the Reiki movement, he studied for decades: meditating, travelling and researching the best way to tap into the universal life force and use it for healing. I followed in his footsteps and did something similar. I learned all kinds of healing techniques and teachings until the true revelation came to me."

"How did you come up with the elixir?" Erica said.

"In a laboratory of course," Arpan replied. "After an equally intense research period and a lot of helpful dreams."

God, this sounded lame and utterly deluded to Erica who rejected his 'divine inspiration' stuff as humbug. If she had not felt such odd sensations while being treated by him she would be laughing at him right now. As if he had read her mind he added: "I don't blame you for keeping a cynical outlook. What we two do here is still beyond comprehension, even for me after all these years."

"What about other illnesses," she asked. "Why did you never heal anything else?"

"That's a very good question. My father died of pancreatic cancer, and my grandfather had diabetes. It seems that organ has a special meaning for me because of them. I developed a particular sense for it. I never liked sugar or sugary things. When I started healing people it was noticeable what great results I had with diabetic patients. The correlation was so significant, it was beyond doubt. Two women who had come to free healing sessions I was holding at a small spiritualist church suddenly had incredible improvements to their blood sugar levels after being treated by me. That is how it all started and of course that pushed me into that specific direction."

"That doesn't answer my question. Why can't you heal, let's say, lung cancer?"

"I wish I knew the answer to that. I tried, but I can only do it if the cancer in the lung is secondary. It caused a lot of criticism in the press and subsequently, doubt."

"I'm not surprised," she said. "It seems very odd."

"It's funny, though," Anuj said. "If a pharmaceutical company produces a cure, a drug or a successful treatment for breast cancer nobody questions them or the product for not having the same effect on bowel cancer. Here, a healer has a special gift and it is brought into disrepute for being too specific."

"I agree," Erica said, "but something about natural energy seems to suggest it should be more universally applicable. However, I totally take your point."

"I had gotten to the stage where I had so many patients I could have worked twice as many hours a day and would have only been able to see a fraction of the people in need. Imagine if I had been able to do more than one type of cancer, it would only have increased the number of disappointed people: there's only so much that one person can do."

"Why did you quit then?" Erica said without thinking.

Arpan immediately pulled back from her and stood up.

"I must rest now, and so should you," he said abruptly and went back inside the dome.

"I wouldn't ask that question again," Anuj said warningly. "He's doing you a huge favour. Leave the past well alone, if you want to continue."

"Are we not done here, yet? I thought this was the last of the treatments. Did he not say he had taken out the cancer cells with his hands? What else could there be left to be done?"

"You've still got a long way to go. He may have killed the cancer, but unless you change your life and heal your soul, the cancer will come back before you know it."

"Oh joy," she sighed, but in a strange way she was pleased. Despite the pain and all the nausea, she felt safe and for once in her life, reassuringly taken care off. She could come here and surrender to the powers of that man and let him work his magic on her. Even despite all of her doubts and trust issues, she realised she needed him and the connection. Returning to civilisation with this vulnerable state of mind seemed too much. It was premature, she felt that clearly, and in her fragile condition far too dangerous.

Chapter 9

She left shortly afterwards, still aching from those imagined 'psychic inner scars'. On the way down to her car she felt a strange sensation, as if she was being watched or followed. It seemed as if her paranoia was going to be the next thing Arpan would need to work on she predicted to herself: about time that got addressed. Her life in the London firm had taught her not to trust people and not to let them too close. Ideas were the top currency in her world and they were often 'copied'.

Stamina and reliability were part of one's most essential skills and so she was always wearing a mask in front of her colleagues. In part it had been an enjoyable game to play but in other aspects it had been hard work. All of her career she had expected betrayals, backstabbing or the leaking of information to the wrong people. Coming to Wales and to this retreat she had assumed her worries would come to an end and with them her defensive manners and frame of mind. However, nosy Mrs Jones did not make that easy, and neither did Anuj or even Arpan's mystery for that matter.

She was just convincing herself that she had nothing to be concerned about when to her surprise she found her car unlocked. It was not like her to forget to lock it: locking things was a reflex action for her. Could she have forgotten? Right now everything was possible. She took a closer look. Clearly nobody had been inside the car, moved or taken anything. Who would bother looking for valuables in such an old banger like this?

At the B&B her unease seemed unjustified. Mrs Jones greeted her politely but almost distantly from the kitchen window and when Erica got to her room she found it unchanged. She had memorised how she had left everything on her desk so could easily tell if the landlady had been snooping around in her absence, but there was no evidence to support her theory.

The odd pulsating sensation from the 'scars' in her body seemed to have ceased at last and physically she felt really good – apart from an inexplicable sense of unease. She saw shadows walking past her window but being on the ground floor and with other guests staying, that was nothing unusual. She wondered if Anuj would see this as something to do with the 'inner child issues' that Arpan had worked on for her when she was 'lost' in the forest.

Her parents had died in a tragic car accident over 22 years ago but that would have nothing to do with Erica's childhood, which she remembered as a happy and content, if a somewhat boring one. Neither popular nor unpopular she had fallen under the radar, had a few respectable boyfriends, got good grades and until the accident seemingly had no drama in her life. 'Inner Child' issues – her arse. Becoming an orphan in your twenties did not count as childhood issues and she had not been abandoned by anyone.

To ease her mind about the sense of being watched she walked up to the window and had a good look around outside. There wasn't anyone visible. No cars and not a trace of the other visitors, yet she could have sworn someone was watching her.

"I'm not surprised you feel that way," Hilda said on the phone, after Erica had decided to call her and get some re-assurance. "Arpan and his thing about secrecy must have rubbed off on you. At the end of the day, the man still is known and a minor celebrity. I could easily trace his whereabouts, so I can't blame him for being worried; others would be able to do the same. He should not put this much pressure on you to keep his secret but instead invest some of your hard earned cash that he so willingly took into a proper security system and effective fencing; that should keep his worries at bay. If the man wants his privacy, he can afford to buy it."

"You're surprisingly forceful today," Erica commented. "Are you quite alright?"

"Of course I am," Hilda said, as though she was not. "It just rubs me up the wrong way that he should be so funny about this when it really is his responsibility. He made you pay through your nose, what else does he want?"

"I must be grateful for what he does, though. He's investing a lot of time and energy into it. Anuj says that it costs Arpan a lot personally to perform his services."

"Who is Anuj?"

"His assistant, did I not mention him before?"

"Not with that name. You know, that it means younger brother in Nepalese. That could add huge further complications, if they are brothers; I hope you realise the implications of that."

78

"It's nothing like that," Erica explained. "Anuj has lost his little brother in a car accident four years ago. I am sure that's why he chose the name. I thought at first that they were father and son but I seriously doubt it. They don't look alike at all. Anuj's mother used to work for Arpan in his heyday. That is their connection. Apparently his mother and Arpan had a huge fight and are still not talking to one another."

"Unless, they fought because he didn't want to have anything to do with his child. It all makes sense, now," Hilda said. "Try and find out the name of his mother," Hilda urged. "That would be worth looking into."

"What are you so bothered about and why are you angry at him, all of a sudden?" Erica wondered. "You got me here and made me commit to it."

"You're not out of the woods, yet. Your lie could still blow up in your face," Hilda said. "It makes perfect sense for me to check the background just a little bit to know what we're dealing with here."

"Do as you please, but I seriously doubt there is anything exciting about the two and their connection," Erica said, very sure of herself. "Arpan seems completely obsessed with his newly found power. I think he isn't taking breaks between sessions because he loves to be that person again. He used to call himself Amesh, a 'Coward Boy', now he calls himself Arpan once more. I think he's back on a massive ego trip or at least amazed at having his powers again. He couldn't care less about Erica Whittaker right now, his mind is elsewhere. I'm almost certain he suspects something like it anyway. He said I looked familiar but never followed it up. A man with his abilities and knowledge... maybe he ignores it to prove a point. That man doesn't think in the same way that we do."

"Nonsense, "Hilda contradicted. "For centuries men have been the same. Whatever clothes they've been wearing and whatever they've been preaching, all were nothing but flesh and blood humans. He does what he does well, but he's not a god. Don't buy into the whole guru act."

"Hilda, I have to thank you for making me do this. I appreciate you so much but I can't deal with your attitude right now, forgive me," Erica said. "I think I'll go for a little walk. The sun is shining and I want to indulge with some warmth on my skin.

"I understand," Hilda said quickly. "You need to keep positive to heal. I'm glad you're having a good time, ignore miserable old me. I don't know what's wrong with me today."

Erica hung up and went for a stroll along the lanes. It was a shame that so many hedges were planted by the side of the road. She couldn't see much of the lush landscape being as short as she was. She found the odd public footpath sign but they often led across fields with horses or sheep, and one even had a bull in it: she didn't feel up for that kind of challenge. At long last she found a viewpoint with a small bench and sat down. She still had the feeling of being followed but that was such an absurd notion around here, where nobody could easily hide, she just had to laugh about it. The sun seemed to do its own healing. She could have fallen asleep in this beautiful setting but weary of her fragile body decided to not take any risks and returned home to the B&B.

She had forgotten her cereal bars in the car, so when she got home she walked to get them. Now this was getting serious; this time she knew for sure that she had locked the doors, but found it unlocked again.

Panicking she ran to her room. At least that door was locked but when she fiddled with her key to open it up she heard a thump from inside. Someone had put the chair under the door handle and the door would not open easily, although it opened a little more each time Erica pushed against it. She banged her fist against the door.

"Open the door. You won't get away. Show yourself," she demanded, to no avail.

She got no reply to any of that. It was a minor miracle that Mrs Jones was not coming to her aid. That woman would not usually miss such action or the excuse for drama, of that Erica was certain and it crossed her mind that this might even be Mrs Jones in there herself. Erica kept pushing against the door and eventually the chair gave way. The window was open, the intruder had escaped already. She rushed towards the window, the place of the mysterious intruder's exit but she could see nobody around.

She leaned out of the window to see if she could hear footsteps but nothing.

Her heart was racing. Who could be after her? Arpan had been in hiding for 20 years. She knew that he was paranoid about his privacy, but honestly, who would care enough about this now, after such a long time? Whoever it was, they could easily walk onto his land and satisfy their curiosity without checking up on her. Or was it Arpan and people associated with him that were trailing her? It seemed equally unlikely since the best time for Arpan's people to check up on her would be while she was with Arpan in the mornings, receiving treatments. None of this made any sense. She looked through her stuff but nothing was taken. Her credit cards, her purse and her document wallet had been with her in her backpack. The intruders had checked her drawers and the closet. There was nothing to be found, which meant that they were likely to come back. The way it had been done didn't look very professional to her. It festered her fears and paranoia but it didn't threaten her too much. In London she had been burgled several times by professionals who had watched her regular moves and knew when to go in and what to take. This had been an amateurish break-in.

She could not afford to make a scene and so decided to keep this to herself. She would have to bite the bullet and ask Mrs Jones to have dinner here tonight, which was an option for the guests. It would enable Erica to have a look at the other guests at the B&B, at least those of them who were also taking the option of a home cooked meal.

"Who else is staying here?" she asked Mrs Jones as casually as she could.

"Look at you coming out of your shell," the landlady said with a broad grin. "I must disappoint you, though. Today you're the only one in the dining room. The other guests are not eating tonight. There are a couple of gays on a hike but 'the boys' are going out into town tonight. Mr Lawlor is staying in his room working on his computer. It will be you and me, my love. What time do you want to eat?"

"What about your husband?"

"He'll eat whenever I tell him to. He doesn't contribute anything in the kitchen, so he has to accept what it dictates. The same as he won't let me have a say with his affairs."

"Good, I will see you at seven then."

Mrs Jones served the promised pasta bake for Erica but she didn't join her guest and instead returned to the kitchen so Erica took her plate and ate the meal in the privacy of her room. She didn't want to leave her room unattended. She wanted whoever had been in her room to know that she was not scared or intimidated, but all night long she woke up from every little noise, of which the countryside had many. She was perturbed that someone had managed to enter her room without a key, although it would not take a master thief to pick as generic a lock as the one her room had. Still, the suspicion remained that either Mrs Jones or one of the other guests was in on it.

What were the intruders after? What could it be about her that would possibly attract such attention from anyone?

In the morning she couldn't wait to get to Arpan and Anuj to tell them about it and see what they would make of it.

Chapter 10

When she got to her usual parking spot at the bottom of the hill she found that another car was parked there already. One of those SUV- wannabes that everyone seemed to drive these days: high off the ground but with no more horse power than a lawnmower. It seemed as if Arpan had a visitor. Erica had to drive on for another few hundred yards until she found somewhere else to park. As she walked up the hill, she heard loud and angry voices arguing violently with one another. One voice sounded like Anuj, the other one belonged to a woman. Maybe it was his mother checking up on him? Erica stopped so that she could hear what the argument was about before walking into the middle of it but she couldn't discern individual words. Cautiously she approached the gate, all the while wondering if she should sit the drama out somewhere out of sight but before she had reached a decision about the best course of action, the gate flew open and a black woman came storming out. She was in her thirties, tall, slim and beautiful, and dressed far too elegantly to be walking up and down a muddy hill in Wales. She stopped for a fraction of a second to look at Erica but then began stomping down the hill as fast as the restrictions of her outfit allowed. Anuj came running after her and although he saw Erica, he was too wrapped up in the moment to seem to care.

"Abby stop! Don't drop a bomb on us like that and then leave," he called out in desperation.

"I have nothing more to say. I've come here to warn you," Abby said angrily, without turning back. "I've done my duty, now it's up to you what to do from here. I'm not getting involved beyond this. It's your mess and you two need to sort it out." With that she stormed out of sight.

Anuj stopped in his tracks and half collapsed hugging one of the trees.

"What was that all about?" Erica asked bewildered. When Anuj didn't respond and kept hugging the tree she realised that this had to be something major. She had never seen him worried; he had always been so confident. For him to show weakness and be worried like this, something had to be seriously wrong.

"Big trouble in little China," he said at last. "Don't worry about it. I'm sorry you had to see this scene. Abby is a big drama queen."

Erica simply nodded. However, when she got to the dome she found Arpan in a rage. He didn't seem to care that Erica was around and could hear him.

"Now the shit has really hit the fan," he said using language Erica would never have expected of him.

"Let's just wait and see," Anuj said half-heartedly.

"It's too late, and you know it. If Abby has found out, then the whole thing must have started already. There won't be anything for us to do now to change that."

"What happened?" Erica asked animatedly.

"Let's just say that the past has caught up with us today," Arpan said sounding devastated.

"You haven't told anyone about what we're doing here, have you?" Anuj asked pointedly.

"Only my secretary from work knows what we're doing, but she's the one who found you in the first place and transferred my funds to you. Why are you asking?"

"It comes down to the whole business of why I'm not practising anymore," Arpan said. "19 years ago I swore to stop all of this for good. Two years ago I broke my promise once for Anuj, a favour I could not refuse for many reasons. I got away with my indiscretion, but with you, I really should have known better than to tempt fate. If certain people got wind of what we're doing here, we will all be doomed."

"Arpan, come on," she said laughingly. "Really, who could possibly mind what you and I do behind closed doors. We are consenting adults, as it were. It's nobody else's business."

"I'm afraid, that's where you're wrong. What we're doing here is of immense importance to someone. I should have known better than to risk what I did. I have put lives at risk to satisfy my own egotistical needs."

"What do you mean?" she asked in disbelief.

"I made a deal with the devil, as it were," Arpan laughed bitterly. "Worse. I made a pact with a pharmaceutical company. Not a bad deal as such, if I'm honest but now that I have broken it, I can't be sure what they'll do."

84

"What kind of deal?" she asked nervously. Was he going to stop her treatment before it was over?

He didn't answer her but paced nervously back and forth in the clearing.

"I wondered how you got away with using the elixir and keep it out of the public eye. There had to be legal implications. What exactly is the elixir?"

"It's something I have discovered and developed over a lengthy period of time," Arpan said to her surprise; she had not expected him to reply at all.

"I hired mighty lawyers to protect its secrecy, so naturally I won't tell you."

"Of course not," she said, nodding her head.

"The pharmaceutical companies wanted to steal it to find out what was in it. When they didn't succeed they offered huge sums to buy it and when they still couldn't get their hands on it with their cash, they tried to have it banned."

"Is that why you stopped practicing, because the elixir would have been banned if you had continued?" Erica asked.

"First of all: I was never forced to stop," Arpan said with irritation in his voice. "I was certainly not ordered by law. I thought of what happened between me and the drug companies as an amusing game of cat and mouse. After word got out about what I was doing and people began to write about it in the papers, suddenly I had a several break-ins at my practice. Why would they pay for it if they could steal it? I didn't have a patent so it was all the more important for them to act quickly, to analyse the content and get a patent for it themselves. You know what a cancer cure is worth: enough to kill for."

"Which makes me wonder all the more why you don't have serious security around here," Erica pointed out. "You couldn't have sold it to the drug company."

"Of course I didn't sell it to them. It wouldn't work without me anyway. It's what I do with my patients once they have the elixir running through their veins that is the vital thing."

"So what happened?"

"All the thieves ever found and got their hands on was a regular saline solution that I left for them to find. They must have been furious about it. My team and I, we all took it rather light-heartedly at first, but when the robbers didn't get what they wanted they came in broad daylight with guns: that was a game changer. We gave them everything we had of course, there was no point in playing the hero. You see, when you are up against that kind of enemy, no security can protect you anyway."

"So they got their hand on the elixir after all?" Erica asked.

"No," he said triumphantly. "They went away with the saline solution as well. The police eventually caught one of the intruders after finding the elixir in his home - amongst other stuff he had stolen. He confessed that someone employed by an international drug company had paid him to steal it."

"You must have been very pleased with yourself," Erica said. "How did you manage to hide your substance from those armed robbers?"

"I'll never reveal that, either," Arpan replied.

"Of course, I understand. What happened to the guy?" she asked.

"He was sentenced for illegal possession of a firearm and some other crimes he had committed, which was how they found him in the first place. There was a little work for me: interviews at the police station, later testifying, etc. I bore him no grudges, he was just trying to make a misguided living."

"Did you sue the drug company behind the break-in?"

"I didn't have time for that. The man never revealed who exactly hired him and I was very busy saving lives; the line of never ending patients seemed somehow much more important. Before long, the drug companies came directly and offered large sums to have a look at my method and the substance. I refused them each time of course."

"There must have been colossal offers for you on the negotiation table. Were you never tempted?" she probed.

"Never. No money in the world could buy my secret. And certainly none from a dubious sources such as that of pharmaceutical companies," Arpan said with disgust.

"They never got the substance," Erica summed up. "What about legal actions?"

"I was never in court," he replied.

"I find that difficult to imagine, since you have no medical licence and no patent or official approval for the substance."

"I was lucky," Arpan said. "One of my first clients was the niece of a well-connected judge. In fact, most of my early clients were from those circles for some reason or the other. It was the initial success stories that bought me friends and support in all the right places. They happily helped me to protect the secret within the legal framework. I disclosed my formula once to an independent and anonymous person who could assert that there was no harm in what I did. All of my clients signed waivers and disclaimer forms – just like you did. Since I had an almost 100% success rate with the people who agreed to my methods, I never had complaints. Everyone but the drug companies was happy."

"There must have been complications, though. There always are." Erica insisted. "This is too good to be true."

"You don't have faith in me?" he said provocatively. "Please, Maria, these people are so predictable, it was an easy game to play."

"They have their powerful friends and henchmen, too," Erica pointed out.

"Yes, they do. If the treatment didn't work, I had people trying to sue me for damage to their bodies. I was also sent people who didn't have cancer with fake documents, I presume only so that they would be injected with the elixir and their blood could be examined: you could tell those people a mile off. Since I had so many applicants and had to turn down people every day so none of them ever knew I had figured them out."

"Are you sure that nobody who had pancreatic cancer was in bed with the drug companies?" she asked.

"Maybe, but let's say that some poor sod was working for them and after his treatment with me that person went straight to their doctors to have themselves examined and searched for traces of my medicine. Nobody would ever have found anything. The substance would already have disappeared."

"How can a substance disappear?" Erica asked fascinated. "With everything that modern medicine can do these days and with the expertise that the drug companies have at their disposal, it seems impossible to imagine they should never have found traces of it."

"If you don't know what you are looking for then you have a very hard job at finding it. Compounds are broken down into other, smaller compounds and by the time someone can get their hands on the blood of one of my patients there is nothing left they can find. Especially if what you are looking for is nothing biologically unusual. I took great enjoyment out of that part," Arpan said and chuckled.

"What about trading and licence issues?" she asked.

"Yes, they came after me too, but I had that certificate that my substance was harmless and so I could repudiate all of those far-fetched claims. Nobody had anything on me.

"If I think about the sums my health insurance had to cough up just to keep us cancer patients alive: the surgeries, the drugs, the pain killers," she said. "If you can stop that, the pharmaceutical companies are missing out on millions and billions of pounds. That must be incentive enough for them to stop you by any means possible."

"That's true. The last resort was a smear campaign in the press, a witch hunt for anything alternative and 'un-proven'. The newspapers claimed that I was nothing but a placebo trickster. There were concerns that people like me deterred patients from seeking professional, western treatment, deluding them into a false sense of security. I never understood how the press managed to milk it for as long as they did, despite the proof they had to the contrary. I know it is hard to comprehend, especially for those who are unwilling to think outside the box and the conventions of that what is measurable scientifically. Unless you can prove and explain how that happened, people can still put it down as a freakish statistical miracle, a mathematical oddity that would not immediately confirm that I had powers or that my substance was legitimate."

"But they stopped you with the contract," Erica said. "Whatever that was."

"Nobody stopped me. It was my decision."

"I am sorry to interrupt," Anuj said, "but we have more pressing matters than your history, Arpan. Maria, can you call your assistant and find out if she spoke to anyone? It's very important that I find out where the leak came from."

"Of course, I'll call her right away." While Erica was fiddling with her phone she told the two men about the intruder to her room last night and her eerie feeling of being followed.

"Could that have anything to do with the drug companies?"

"Possibly," Arpan said, "although they would probably come directly here to challenge me. I'm afraid that your people are something else, and that's not good news either. I hope they were just regular thieves, maybe some local potheads looking for cash. Whatever it is, that has probably nothing to do with us. Are you in any kind of trouble?"

"Not that I know of," she replied and dismissed his comment for now. She had too much to think about already and would deal with the mystery of her stalkers later. Erica tried all of Hilda's numbers but the woman was unreachable.

"It'll have to wait until she gets my messages."

Arpan didn't seem interested in her problems.

"We need damage control," he said to Anuj. "Maybe if I come clean they will let this one slide. We've been keeping it pretty low profile so there is really no damage done. They must appreciate that."

"Yes, but look how agitated Abby was. That should give you an indication of how huge this could become," Anuj said.

"What damage?" Erica asked anxiously. "You have to tell me about that deal."

"That would be another breach of the agreement itself," Arpan informed her. "It doesn't matter. Just keep trying your assistant."

"You told Anuj about the deal," she pointed out. "I'm involved, too, whether either of us like it or not. It is better if I know."

"Anuj knows about the deal because of his mother," Arpan replied. "That had actually nothing to do with me. I would never have told him. The less people know, the less complicated things will be for all of us. Trust me, it's best for you if you genuinely don't know."

"You sound so dramatic," Erica said dismissively. "If I didn't know you any better as a spiritual person I would call you deluded and a weird conspiracy theorist."

"Enough," Anuj told her angrily. "What are we going to do about her?" he asked Arpan.

"I have to finish what I started, haven't I?" Arpan replied. "If I get punished for what I did, at least I did one thing right. Get the injection ready, we don't have time to lose. There are not many more treatment sessions left to do anyway."

"You're mad," Anuj said, shaking his head but he didn't argue his case any further.

Erica let her body sink back in relief. All through her discussion with Arpan she had been so worried about the treatment finding an abrupt and premature ending, before it had taken and healed her. The treatment had become something of an addiction for her, a daily infusion of hope and the promise of a future. She didn't care anymore about anything beyond that. What was it that the drug companies could do to her or Arpan that was so bad? They wouldn't kill anyone, or else they would have done that a long time ago.

"Come in to the dome," Arpan said. "At least we can do it in privacy there."

"The pancreas balances a lot of hormones," he explained to her. "The sweetness of life is in her hands. That's what has come out of balance for you. Today I'm going to work on your attitude towards life and on your hormonal glands. It will probably get you quite hysterical and confused. I must warn you that if you're going to be in too unreasonable a state after the treatment, I will have to restrain you until you're more agreeable."

"Anything you think necessary," she agreed. Strapped to the massage table she received her injection. The burning sensation was very mild. Arpan spoke to her in a lulling voice, making her breathe into her stomach and asking her to visualise a dark tunnel that she willingly walked into within the realms of her mind. He counted back from 10 as he made her visualise going down a steep spiral staircase further down into the darkness.

She drifted off somewhere around then and couldn't remember anything that had happened when she woke up. All she noticed for now was a raging anger at being tied to the table.

"Get me off the table," she demanded, but she soon realised that she was alone in the dome and nobody came to her aid. She called for Arpan and Anuj but they didn't come and she soon gave up. Time seemed endless as she was waiting and she really needed to use the facilities, too. Where were the guys? How dared they abandon her like this?

"Arpan!" she called out. "Anuj, come here and let me go."

Anuj came running into the dome and motioned her to silence. He looked seriously scared and clearly meant it. She could feel the rush of hormones Arpan had spoken of but got herself under control and complied. Anuj slowly undid her straps.

90

"We have visitors," he whispered. "You need to get out of here, quickly."

He grabbed her by the hand and led her to the entrance to the dome. He took a quick peek outside and quickly retracted his head.

"They are here already," he explained in even more of a whisper. "We need to be very careful. When I pull on your hand you have to follow me really quickly outside and then I'll lead you behind the dome so we can escape without being seen."

"Okay," she agreed.

He took her by the hand and peeked outside of the dome. Then he suddenly jumped out and pulled her after him. Without looking behind she followed him as instructed and the two of them continued running away from the dome for several minutes until she ran out of breath. They carried on walking until they reached another gate.

"If you go down this path you will come to the place where you parked your car today," Anuj said abruptly. "See you tomorrow!"

He closed the gate and made his way back to the dome. Erica stood at the other side of the gate, stunned and confused. Angry and disorientated she was overpowered by her emotions and unwilling to comply. She had no intentions of going back to the B&B and wasting another day worrying and wondering what was going on. This nonsense had to stop now, she decided. She would find out what the big secret was. Didn't she have a right to know what she was up against? She slowly opened the gate and made sure there was no sign of Anuj before making her way back to the dome where she hoped to eavesdrop on Arpan and his visitors. The closer she came to the dome, the more careful she treaded. At last she got there and she could make out the voices of the two men and some visitor easily.

"Julia, this was a once-off," she heard Arpan explain. "I swear. One person, one very discreet case. It was nothing more than a singular momentary weakness of my mind. My innate desire to help one more person got the better of me. Can't you imagine how hard it is for me not to help? It's not the beginning of anything new and not a re-opening of the past. I'm committed to the contract. I just couldn't help myself with this one. She found me and I felt sorry for her."

The petty and shrill voice of a determined woman replied with no trace of sympathy. "That is not what we agreed upon. 'Just this once' is already too much. You know the implications and repercussions from this. Your patient may promise discretion all she wants, but where do we have guarantees? I made some enquiries and the fact of the matter is, that she's a hedonistic party girl who enjoys her drinks. Let her go out with her friends and get drunk – don't you think at some stage she's going to go bragging about how she beat cancer? Let one of her drinking partners tell the press and the whole thing is reopened."

"I'll make sure that won't happen," Arpan tried to calm the woman down.

"Do you want us to pull out of our commitment? Would you like it if we decided to skip a few months' payments? We pay dearly for the deal."

"I know, and I'm so very grateful for it. The idea of saving a life with my own hands got me intoxicated and carried away."

"You're saving lives all the time," Julia said, a little gentler now. "Within the parameters of your beliefs, you're saving lots of lives every day by making us do what we do at our end of the deal. In fact, you're saving many more than you could do so by your 'treatments'. Never forget that."

"Why is Maria so important to you?" Arpan asked.

"Your 'Maria' can bring back the interest in your elixir," the woman replied.

Erica wondered what the woman looked like. She pictured her as either a thin-lipped business woman in a power suit, or a bespectacled, wart riddled monster? The incarnation of evil by the sounds of her. Erica slowly inched her way forward to the edge of the dome and risked a quick look. It was the latter: a woman with jeans and a red anorak, hardly looking like a business executive, even though she clearly was. Julia had short dark hair in no discernible style, she wore glasses and had a terrible set of teeth. Maybe that was why she was so harsh: ridiculed and bullied at school, always overlooked by the other sex, wrapped up in a fear of being disadvantaged and determined to pay back the world for everything she had missed out on.

"You refused to sell us the formula," Julia added accusingly, snapping Erica out of her dreaming. "You're the one stopping it from reaching a wider audience, Arpan, we would love to mass produce it. You really have a responsibility to society to do so, don't you think?"

"The elixir won't work on its own, it would be useless in your hands," Arpan defended himself. "I have told you that many times."

"Oh nonsense," the woman brushed him off. "I'm not one of your gullible hippy friends. Don't try to lull me in with your speech about your magical healing powers. I'm a scientist and at some level you must be one, too. You and I know it's the formula of that injection that does the work. You're not a godsent messiah."

"You'd sue me if I gave you the formula and it proved my point that it won't work on its own," Arpan said confidently.

"Try me. We could do great things with the elixir. Drug companies are good, they help. We're no monsters, Arpan. Public opinion discredits us but we are working our arses off every day to cure diseases and to make people's lives more bearable. We can't help it that the market forces favour us. You may call us selfish for making a profit but we reinvest much of that money into research. We don't deserve the bad press we're getting. Give me the formula and we can forget all about your patient."

"No." Arpan said calmly.

Julia stomped her foot on the ground.

"Why are you being such a stubborn egotistical man? My predecessors warned me about you but it defies belief. We could wipe pancreatic cancer off the earth, something you couldn't do by yourself. Not this way."

"You couldn't do that and I can't do it either," he said, the resignation clear in his voice. "I can't give you the formula."

"We could reach a number of people beyond your imagination. Don't they all deserve to be healed?" she pushed him further.

"I would love doing that, but I can't because it won't work on its own."

"In that case I need to address the main reason for my being here: if you're stubborn and aren't sticking to our agreement then we will have to think very carefully about the consequences, too. It's only fair. Abby keeps a close tab on us, she knows that we are strictly keeping our end of the bargain and we still do, despite your recent activities. But if we cannot trust you anymore? Who knows how many people you actually have been treating behind our back!"

"Nobody, I swear," Arpan said. "Let's forget about this. Now that you've tracked me down, you can easily monitor what I do."

"It's not that simple. We always knew where you lived and could keep tabs on you if we wanted," Julia said smugly.

"Well, then you must know that I've done nothing apart from this one case this week," Arpan replied.

"Let me make a different point," Julia said. "A simple calculation, Arpan: add all the medical bills of all the cancer patients you were healing each week and you know how much cash we are earning from keeping you out of practice. Compare that sum to the money we spend for the orphanages in Africa and you can see how generous we are. Then think of how many lives you saved each week and then count how many of those little buggers we save from starvation or AIDS every week."

"That is misrepresentation. It misses out the money I used to get from my clients, or rather, the charities I gave the money to are missing out from my loss of income. I can save additional lives with that."

"Maybe the number of lives saved is similar," Julia said. "But the world is a different place now than it was twenty years ago. If you begin practising again, you would have watchdogs and trading standard commissioners on your back on a much larger scale. If Labour had been in government, they would have introduced new legislation purely for the sake of getting their hands on your money and they would have stopped your exorbitant fee charging. You have no idea what would have happened if you had continued your practice in the way you did then. In the long run, someone would have brought you down: we did you a huge favour. The money would have gone to the tax man and not to charities so at least you managed to get yourself very rich before all of that happened. I appreciate that you were well connected and protected, but in the longer term you would have run into problems larger than you can imagine."

"I made one tiny mistake," Arpan pleaded. "I let myself be seduced into helping her out."

"It's not that simple," Julia said sharply. "It proves that you are still producing the elixir, which is against our arrangement.

94

That woman has been noticed, people are talking about her and her story around here. It won't be long before someone connects the dots and suddenly we have a news story. This has got to stop right here."

"What do you want me to do?"

"That woman must never be healed. You make sure she dies of her cancer as per her medical history. If she doesn't die, you'll have a bunch of African children on your conscious. And that is letting you off lightly."

"I've already treated her and she has no more cancer cells left in her body."

Julia snorted: "We need to get hold of her then. Her medical records must not be able to prove another 'miracle'. You will need to bring her to us." Julia demanded.

"What are you going to do with her?" Arpan asked concerned.

"Examine her, make sure she still has cancer, or at least touch up her medical records one way or another. We will think of something. If you're the magician that you claim to be, then you better give her back the cancer that was hers. Or else there will be dead children in Africa."

"I can't do that," Arpan said with despair in his voice. "I can't make that decision, and neither can you. It's inhumane. You can't blackmail me like this."

"I think I just did, Arpan," Julia said triumphantly. "Maybe you will feel better if I told you that she only recently changed her name to Maria Miller. Such an unimaginative name, I expected better of her."

"So what?" Arpan said irritated.

"Her real name is Erica Whittaker," she paused for effect. "Not much of a psychic are you, if you didn't even notice that. Maybe that little and vital piece of information will help persuade you."

Erica wished she could have seen Arpan's face and his reaction to the mention of her real name, but he was standing with his back towards her.

"I personally would much prefer to avoid a public scene or abduction charges," Julia added. "If she came to our lab in Munich voluntarily, that would be the best solution. Think about what she did, and about your pet children in Africa. Let Abby know a soon as you get this whole thing sorted, ok?"

"Julia, there must be another way," Arpan said. "I never harmed another human being."

"With all the 'healing' you did, it won't matter. You're still going to heaven or nirvana or wherever you believe in. I'll show myself out."

Chapter 11

Erica's heart was racing. Arpan had not known about her. Her worries in that regard had been unfounded and he had done everything for her with the best of intentions and without any ambiguous feelings. But that had all changed, he knew about her now and that could change things drastically, and so close to the finishing line. Would he continue with his healing or tell her to go to hell? Would he deliver her to that devil woman? What would be his true colours? In a way, nothing and everything had changed at the same time. Should she run? Did she still have time, and if so, where could she run to? She really ought to have it out with him and have a frank discussion about everything. It was a big risk and he was now no longer entirely trustworthy. How the sins of her youth had finally caught up with her, 18 years later.

It sounded as if Julia had left the property, it was eerily quiet all of a sudden. Where were Anuj and the dog? Erica waited and listened for a noise of some kind that might give her an indication of what was happening on the other side of the dome. Maybe the men were meditating? Ideally, she needed there to be noise and distraction so that she could retreat to the other gate undetected and get to her car. Right now she couldn't trust anyone. Was it safe to stay at the B&B with that woman after her? Just because Julia and her people hadn't found or approached Erica there yet, didn't make the place safe. She needed Arpan to finish the treatment, she had to have an honest conversation with him, maybe after he had a chance to cool down and digest the information of who she really was. She sat uncomfortably in her spot for a long time until she decided that Arpan had to have left with the woman. She had not heard the tiniest of noise. She got up and very slowly started to make her way as quietly as she could into the forest. In her mind, every step she took seemed to make a huge noise, but in reality it was only the smallest crackle from a twig. She seemed in luck and got almost to the gate when she bumped into Anuj and Ashank who ran excitedly up to her as usual.

"I had a feeling you might decide to stay," Anuj said calmly. "I noticed your car was still here. Is the show over now? Has Julia left?"

"Yes, just a few minutes ago, and I really should be going, too," Erica said, visibly uncomfortable.

"What did you hear?" he asked her.

"More than I wanted to," Erica said. "I'm sure Arpan will tell you all about it."

"On the contrary, I'm sure he won't tell me anything about the conversation. Go on, bring me up to scratch."

Erica hesitated at first but then she thought that maybe she could find an ally in Anuj in all of this.

"In a nutshell: they demand that he stops seeing me and that he hands me over to their labs for tests, like a guinea pig or a lab rat. I'm not going to take my chances with that, so I'm off. Tell him I said goodbye and I'll be in touch."

Erica tried to get past Anuj, but he touched her shoulder gently and got her to turn around and face him.

"He'll never turn you in," he reassured her. "You don't have to worry about that. You're really funny sometimes."

"Julia made a pretty convincing case," Erica pointed out, "and she has some leverage and hold over him."

"Arpan is committed to the process now," Anuj tried to convince her. "He can't simply abandon ship and 'hand you over' to her company for tests. I don't know what you think of him but you're clearly mistaken. He would never cave, even under pressure. That's who he is, and nothing will change that."

"The deal with the drug company seemed pretty important to him, enough to make him give up the healing twenty years ago."

"He made a conscious decision at that time and did what he thought was best then. I know he would never compromise his integrity by giving into threats."

"Well, sometimes there are choices forced upon you where you have to choose the lesser of two evils," Erica said. "She just put him in that position and logic demands that he caves for the greater good. I can't blame him. "

"All I know is that Arpan needs to finish the treatment," Anuj assured her. "He has fully committed himself to the process. The way he works and heals, he cannot simply pull out of it halfway through. His energy has merged with yours and he would pay a high personal price if he stops right now. Whatever they demand, he won't comply."

"Apparently if he delivers me, the company will continue their charitable work in his name and save lots of children's lives in Africa. If he doesn't, they pull out of their commitment because he is in breach of their contract. By 'sacrificing' me he will enable more lives to continue. It is a no brainer, even for me."

"That's a nasty proposition and evil blackmail," Anuj uttered angrily. "I had no idea. This contract runs out in six years and after that the company is legally bound to continue their end of the bargain while he's free to practice again. We're so close to the finishing line."

"Exactly, so why spoil it now for my sake? Those six years represent a long time and a lot of African lives," Erica pointed out "He'll want to save the children, I'm certain of it. He'll sacrifice me; he would probably sacrifice himself like he sacrificed his profession for them twenty years ago."

"I doubt it," Anuj said. "He wasn't called 'Coward Boy' for nothing," he added.

"What do you mean by that?"

"Nothing, forget I said that. Healing is all he lives for. Look at him: no wife, no children, nothing but meditation and healing. He lives so that others can live. He's often regretted that he made the deal with Julia's predecessor. He bargained with lives and he probably did the right thing. His money couldn't have made the same impact as the policy decisions of a drug cartel. He was right to do so but it left him crippled and full of self-doubt; frustrated that he was reduced to this mundane living."

"How did that make him a coward?" Erica asked.

"He lost his confidence. His initial success rate of 100% shrank. When he had a bad run of people dying despite the healing, it made him vulnerable and in the end he took the deal. During the last 20 years he has tried to be as clean and pure and healthy as he can be, so when he returns to the healing profession he will be the best possible vessel of unspoilt energy that he can be. He could have lived in Las Vegas or in the Caribbean if he was that kind of person, but instead he decided to stay here in the dome."

"How is that supposed to comfort me? The equations of lives saved are still against me," Erica pointed out. "Julia didn't give him much of a say or a choice in the matter."

"Julia only dealt with Amesh, the coward. She never met him when he was Arpan. Now that he has his strength back and his willpower, he will come up with a solution."

"I think I should turn myself in. If I don't go voluntarily, they'll find me. They know my name and my history. I have nowhere to run, not with cancer in my body anyway."

"Let's speak to Arpan. He will know what to do," Anuj said and headed for the dome.

"Sorry, I'm not coming with you. I better take my fortune in my own hands," she said and began walking in the opposite direction.

"Maria, he needs to finish his work with you. He can do it without Julia ever knowing."

"Thanks, but Julia is on our case now. She'll find us before he's finished the job. I can't trust Arpan any longer. Julia said to Arpan she would prefer not to risk a scandal by abducting me in the eye of the public. How can we be really sure of that?"

"Then trust me and what I say. I'm on your side, Maria, and Arpan is too. I'll never enter negotiations with blackmailers and neither will he."

"I can't," Erica said. "There is more to this," she struggled for the next words to come out. "My name is not Maria. I changed it before I came here so you wouldn't know my true identity. There is history between me and Arpan that will change the entire situation."

"I promise you, I will protect you. Let's have an honest discussion with Arpan." When she didn't reply to this he added: "It's like you said earlier, Julia and her team know where you live; if they are determined enough they'll find you. You must speak to Arpan, there are no two ways about it. You know that, too."

She sighed. He was right of course. It was time everything came out into the open but when they got to the dome it was deserted: Arpan was nowhere to be seen.

"He hasn't taken anything with him," Anuj observed. "I guess he went for a walk to clear his mind."

"To be honest, I'm quite pleased he's not here," Erica said. "It gives me more time to think."

100

"You're so dramatic sometimes," Anuj said with a silly grin on his face.

Well, she thought, it wasn't his life on the line.

Arpan joined them an hour later. His face was pale and clearly showed the inner torment he was going through.

"I'm glad you're here," he said to Erica. "I really need to speak to you."

"I know," she said. "I eavesdropped on you talking to Julia."

"In that case we don't have that much talking to do," he corrected himself, looking stern all the same.

"No?" she asked confused and surprised. How could he be so forgiving and generous?

"No. Let the past be our past," he said convincingly magnanimous. "What I need to do is to give you another treatment and I need to do it fast. It's a bit risky to do it now but I see no other option. Today I guess I have time for deliberations, but come tomorrow I have no idea what Julia will decide to do. I must complete your course right away. I've been thinking about it ever since Julia left and I feel good about it now. Anuj, get the injection ready. Maria, you come with me."

Anuj looked triumphant at her. "I told you so!"

She wondered why Arpan had called her Maria when he knew her real name was Erica. She decided to take it as a sign that he would treat her as the person he had met and decided to heal, rather than the person that she had once been and who had caused him so much grief. It was true, though, she was not that Erica anymore. She had changed from the woman whose path had crossed Arpan's once and she was not even the same person than she was a few days ago. Everything was so different.

Inside the dome Arpan told Anuj to leave him and his patient alone and the young man happily obliged.

"Good luck!" Anuj said with a wink and left.

"Why are you being so nice to me?" Erica asked Arpan when they were alone.

"I committed myself to you and to the healing," he replied gently. "It's against my nature to do anything else. Only if you chose something without compromising, like I've done with my entire life, can you become what I've become. Maybe this is why I never got to heal other cancers, because I could only throw enough energy into the one cause and not split it into two or more."

"You compromised it 20 years ago when you gave it all up," she pointed out.

"That's right," he admitted. "I had very good reasons, though, and meditated on it for a long time. It was the right thing to do then and I don't regret that decision. I feel the situation has changed since then. Listen. I will heal you today. You will contact the drug cartel on your own terms when you've recovered and will endure the tests they perform on you. After all, they cannot bring the cancer back. I told Julia honestly that I hadn't healed you yet, but after today you will be healed completely. They will know how long you've been in the area and, compared to the way I used to administer the treatment, will assume that you haven't gotten the full course yet. We are safe for another few days before she would consider the treatment complete. The worst case scenario is that she has positioned her henchmen around your B&B and the compound here to make sure neither of us gets away; as far as she is concerned there is no urgency in getting you. We have time."

Erica sighed with relief. "Thank God." All she cared for was to have the treatment finished. After that, what could possibly happen to her?

"Once Julia has done her tests she will make you sign some nondisclosure forms, you might even get a nice lump sum from it. You'll have six years to watch your health and have regular scans to monitor your pancreas. After that I can see you as a patient again without any repercussions. That way we all will live happily ever after. Of course I will return your money to you, so you can pay for those regular private examinations if needed."

"Thank you," she said and smiled at him with admiration and disbelief at such goodness.

Arpan strapped her to the table and administered another injection. She noticed that the liquid this time had a different colour, not as blue as usual, and when there was no burning sensation she looked questioningly at Arpan; unlike before, she felt terribly drowsy.

"What have you done," she asked him as her speech garbled. "You tricked me!" she accused him.

"Trust me," she heard him say. "Trust me." Then she passed out.

When she came to she was no longer in the dome. It took her a while to come to her senses and before she could see anything in the darkness. She found herself lying on a single mattress in the middle of a very small room. She guessed it was a pantry or a room in a basement or something similar to it. Only gradually could she make out the exact outlines. This was most definitely a basement; there was the tiniest of windows at the top of the room with iron bars and a view to a grassy surface. She could see a little reflection of pale light. At least the moon was still as strong as it had been a few days ago, which helped her to get familiar with her new surroundings.

That rat, she thought. Arpan had tricked her into letting him sedate her, and then he had incarcerated her. Her number was up now, game over. He might as well have killed her. That drug bitch would come and get her. Spiritually evolved? Right. Arpan was as easily bought as every other human being on the planet. How could she have fallen for such an old trick? She wondered if it was possible for the drug company to insert cancer cells into her, so that her medical records would show she was still suffering from cancer. Whatever they were planning to do, they'd make sure that Erica wouldn't live to tell.

How naïve she'd been to believe that Arpan could leave their past in the past. He obviously hadn't forgiven her and Anuj had been mistaken about the 'tie' between the healer and his patient. All of this was just a big show.

She lay back down and her heart sank. She had come so close to be healed, so close to the end of the treatment. Why did it have to go wrong at the last moment? Was it Mrs Jones who had ratted on her? Had she snooped through Erica's documents and drawn the right conclusions? It seemed beyond her capacity, but then again, busybodies always found the weak spot and made sure they did the worst with it. It was very possible. Had Hilda's investigations tripped an alarm bell somewhere?

Had Anuj known about all of this and only pretended to be her friend in order to lure her back to the dome? He had promised to protect her. Days of building up the all-important trust had been flushed down the drain. She didn't believe anything anymore. She didn't have to. The facts spoke their own language.

"Hello?" she called out after a while of dwelling on her negative thoughts. "Anyone? Who's there?" she shouted but nobody answered her.

"Help, get me out of here!" she shouted louder, again and again, but nothing and nobody stirred. She could smell the grass and the trees and suspected that she was still somewhere in the vicinity to Arpan and his dome. Captive in a holding cell, it was all clear to her now.

Her head was thumping, a side effect of the sedative she reckoned. She hoped she wouldn't be sick because the damp smell in here was already not the greatest. Eventually she fell asleep again until the morning sun woke her up. She continued with her shouts for help but the lack of response was very disheartening and her vocal cords began to hurt. There seemed no point in continuing with it. She had to save her voice and wait for the inevitable.

Not too long after she heard footsteps above her but suddenly her courage left her and instead of calling out to draw attention to herself she thought it wiser to listen to the sounds first. She was relieved when a trap door in the ceiling opened and once her eyes had adjusted to the light coming from above, she recognised the familiar and surprisingly friendly face of Anuj.

"Good morning, Maria," he said as if this locking her in was nothing. "Hope you're feeling better now." He carefully put a ladder down for her.

"Come on up when you're ready."

She couldn't believe it. She was free to leave her prison. What on earth was all this about?

"Where are we?" she asked confused, looking around herself as she climbed up the little ladder. She was feeling a little woozy but strong enough to make it without fear of falling down. She found herself in a tiny wooden cottage, no bigger than a summer house and far too small to suggest a basement underneath it.

"Kind of a safe house if you will," he said and chuckled. "We're still on Arpan's property, just a little remote to keep you out of sight."

"I never saw this when we walked around the grounds," she observed.

"Technically we are outside the grounds you know but the land adjacent to his compound belongs to Arpan, too," Anuj explained.

"Of course, he must have made a killing in his day," she said. "I'm still amazed that he's limited to such modest conditions. If I were him I'd live quite differently."

"The land was all his, or his family's, long before he became famous. He bought this cottage later but through an agent and under a different name, so it looks as if these are two separate properties and owners. We're safe here from Julia and her minions."

She scanned the room a little more carefully. There was a sofa, a chair and a small desk. No electricity or artificial lights.

"Remind me again, why I'm here and not in the dome?" she asked. "I'm hardly untraceable here and my car is still parked near here, for anyone to see."

"I took care of your car," Anuj said. "We needed one anyway. Nobody knows you're here."

"The woman at the B&B might make some noise about this," Erica pointed out. "She has taken a huge interest in me and what I do."

"Yes," Anuj said. "She's probably the one who called Julia in the first place but she won't raise any more alarms now. Her job is done."

"How can you be sure of it? What happens when I don't go back to her B&B? They'll start looking for me and will be back here before you know it. Why else would I be in the 'safe house'?"

"Julia won't find you here. Besides, she believes in the elixir, else she wouldn't keep running after it. She trusts that you are cancer free now and of course that makes it only logical for you to return to your flat and to your job and continue with your life as if nothing ever happened. Agreed? She won't worry about you running off. According to Arpan's usual treatment plan she still has a while before she should get worried."

"You sound very confident," Erica said.

"You have watched too many conspiracy movies by the sound of you," he replied. "She can't afford to get her hands dirty; she can solve the case in other ways. You have nothing to fear from her. Arpan was right when he told you that all she's going to do is falsify your records and pay you off."

"It seems an awful lot of effort to silence one man and his healing ability," Erica pointed out.

"That's true," Anuj said. "What she's really after is the elixir itself. Amesh guaranteed her a first buyer's option if he ever should sell the formula. It makes good business sense for her to keep it out of the limelight to avoid a bidding war. Her company speculates that Arpan will sell the formula to them before he dies, or the benefactor of his will afterwards. Then they will make huge returns for their investment. They can patent it and use it for 25 years, let alone the help in research for other cancers. The potential is huge. Keeping his reputation muddy is part of their strategy. They need people to forget about him and think that Arpan was a figment of their imagination. There are plenty of people around who were healed by him but their stories are in the past and forgotten. Any of them could come back and there is nothing Julia can do about that thread. A new success story would be very upsetting but not the end of the world. If you behave and cooperate they won't press the matter any further."

"If that were so, then why am I here in a safe house?" Erica asked once more, very aggressively. "You're making a convincing case but it isn't your life that's at stake."

"We have more angles to cover," Anuj explained. "There are all kinds of people who may take an interest in the elixir: other healers, and criminals who want to steal it and use it for their own means. If the woman from the B&B got wind of it and mentioned it to Julia, she may have told other people. You said she was a busybody. They tend to tell their stories to more than one person."

"That threat must have been around from day one. If Mrs Jones knew about Arpan, then she could have leaked that information long before now. It doesn't make sense."

"I'm afraid it doesn't," he admitted. "We're just speculating. Julia showing up here could attract attention from other people who might be watching her."

"How come you never bothered to install more security?" Erica asked. She was gradually feeling better, the headache was still there but not as intense anymore. She just couldn't understand how amateurish Arpan was behaving in light of such huge threats.

Anuj on the other hand seemed very defensive and angry at her for her challenging attitude.

"For the same reason," he said sharply. "It would only attract attention if we had such systems in place, people would start asking questions who Arpan is and they might find out; then think of the people we're up against, no alarm system could stop them."

"You were worried enough about security to hide me here and lock me up," she pointed out. "I can't say that I'm very impressed with that. I was really scared waking up here."

"I'm sorry for the dramatic appearance and for locking you in," he said sheepishly. "We had to leave you behind while sorting out some admin, as it were. We set a trail that will get any stalker of yours away from here. It will give us a considerable amount of time to get ourselves organised. We knew the sedative you were given would last for a few hours, especially in your weakened state."

"Why a sedative at all? Was that a date rape drug or something?" She was quite angry.

"To finish the treatment off so quickly Arpan had to be very forceful with his energy and he said he couldn't put you through it while you were conscious. It would have been too painful so close after the other treatment."

"I could have done with some sedation during the other sessions," she said half-jokingly.

"I can imagine," he said.

"So are we in danger or not?"

"For now you needn't worry, we've got it all covered."

"How can I not worry?" she asked outraged.

"I appreciate that," he replied. "What puzzles us more than anything is what has been happening at the B&B. The break-in, the people following you, none of that makes sense; that's not how Julia operates: it's very suspicious."

"I refuse to believe that the B&B break in has anything to do solely with me and my private life. I pose no threat to anyone, especially since I left my job with more or less complete certainty that I would be dead within a few weeks. I may have enemies there but they would hardly bother me now."

"What about people gaining something from you while you are still alive?" Anuj said. "You know, inheritance etc. Who would be getting your money?"

She laughed out loud.

"Money?" You have to be kidding me," she replied. "You saw my money. I have 12.03% of it left. You're gaining from it. That's it. I have no relatives or close friends left, I'm leaving my money to a charity."

"Is there anyone who would think they are owed your inheritance? A friend, a former spouse?"

"Not that I can think of. My two exes are so much better off than me, they wouldn't waste their time on such a little sum."

"What about your assistant?" he asked.

"She led me to you and has full access to my accounts and money. She could have transferred all of it to Switzerland if she wanted. The people spying on me must be after you."

"Arpan will be back soon. He was trying to connect with some of his old contacts so he might have found out something."

"I'm starving," she changed the subject. "Where's my backpack? I have some cereal bars in there."

"Over there," he said and pointed to a corner behind him. "You'll need your strength. You're in for another session this morning."

"You're joking?" she said. "I can't take another one. He's going to kill me with this."

"There is no way around it," Anuj said sternly. "We're running out of time. If he wants to complete the treatment uninterrupted, then today is the best and possibly only day for it. Until we know who's interested in either of us besides Julia it's best to carry on. Your car is on the way to Scotland, driven by a woman looking much like you. That might throw any people trailing you off your scent."

"I know that I agreed to trust you and to let you do what you have to do, but I still don't know what you injected me with all those times and especially yesterday. I can't even remember anything about the last treatment. I'm very worried about his suggestion that I should hand myself over to the drug company. I heard that woman say that they want me to die of cancer to keep up appearances."

"Now you are back at your conspiracy theories," Anuj laughed. "If they'd wanted to they would have killed Arpan and you by now; they don't want that kind of complication. Julia is a control freak and from what Arpan told me, she prefers to handle things herself, however challenging they are."

"It would be a lot easier if I was dead so there's no proof of Arpan's abilities," Erica pointed out. "I'm scared they can plant fresh cancer cells in my body just so that my medical records show that I'm still ill."

"That is a very far-fetched idea." Anuj laughed at her paranoia. "I don't think you can create cancer like that, and even if they injected you with some cancer cells it wouldn't help. Arpan has healed you, and you should be immune to such cancer cells. Secondly, any scans would show a different tumour than the one that you originally had. It would never wash. Thirdly, there would be traces from their operation. This is ridiculous."

"I would be calmer if it wasn't my life on the line."

"I appreciate that," he said, "but your fears are quite irrational."

"I don't think they are. Arpan's problems would disappear if I were to disappear, too. Now I find myself locked away in a safe house."

"You are free to go," Anuj said, getting up and opening the door wide. "I'm sorry we gave you the wrong impression. Please leave if that is what you want to do. We're holding you here to help you and certainly not against your will. It's in your interest to complete the treatment. Say the word and we'll get the car back here in no time."

"Can't you see my problem? If I leave now, I might not be cured. If I stay, who is to say that Arpan might not undo what he did for me?" Erica said and began to well up.

"He promised," Anuj said calmly.

"That was before we were found out and before he knew who I was. You cannot blame me for being a little concerned. The situation has changed and immediately Arpan knocked me out with a sedative. He has a good reason to hate me personally."

"You're underestimating him and his infinite compassion," Anuj said. "Whatever you have done to him, he has forgiven you. I can assure you of that."

"Julia made him choose between me and the life of orphans. You know about the deal. Of course he must choose the larger number of human lives to save. I know you said that his energy is linked to mine and that he could not sacrifice me without harming himself, but maybe he has managed to separate the link between us while I was unconscious. I know nothing of the powers he possesses. It's impossible to trust him."

"He wouldn't do anything to get blood on his hands. If confronted with a choice where either option will bring someone to harm, he will simply do nothing. He will not say yes to one murder to prevent several others or vice versa. He won't be drawn into it. Full stop."

"Has he told you who I am?"

"No, but I doubt that that makes any difference to him."

"Does the name Whittaker mean anything to you?"

"It means a lot to me," Anuj said calmly.

"I'm Erica Whittaker."

Anuj didn't respond with the vehemence she had expected. He only looked at her with sad eyes.

"I can see why you think that this would change the situation, but not with Arpan," he reassured her. "Arpan is forgiveness."

She hoped this was true.

When Arpan came back he looked calm and not in the least worried.

"Any news?" Anuj asked him.

Arpan shook his head and without further ado he produced a syringe.

"This is a different colour," Erica blurted out. She could swear that the liquid was more green than blue. "What is this?"

"It's the last injection," Arpan said casually.

"That doesn't look like the other injections," she said, shaking her head and stepping back. "Arpan, what are you doing?"

Arpan looked genuinely surprised at her outburst.

"The elixir has always looked like this. Your mind is playing tricks on you, if anything. Anuj, tell her."

"No, it was green, not blue," Erica insisted.

"Arpan is right," Anuj confirmed. "It has always had that blue-green colour, you just have never had a good look at it. For heaven's sake, stop your paranoia."

"I am sure the liquid was a different type of green," she insisted. "I'm not having that."

"In that case my work here is done," Arpan said. "Think about it carefully. It will leave you vulnerable to the cancer coming back. Given your tense nature that might well be very soon. You would be relying on continuous scans to see if it has come back."

"I'll need those scans in any case," she said. "For the rest of my life."

"You won't need them if I complete the treatment. My healing ends the cancer for good. Now breathe," he said. "Take a moment to relax. You know deep down in your heart that I am your friend. Look at me and try to take in my energy. You'll see for yourself that there is no intention of any harm from me."

He took her hand and squeezed it gently. She couldn't stop looking into his eyes, it was like a hypnotic draw. She felt very tired all of a sudden but tried to fight against it.

"I don't know who to trust now," she said worriedly.

"You have no choice," Anuj told her bluntly. "This is your last chance. If you don't take it the tumour will return with absolute certainty. You need this."

"I don't know…" she said, her resistance weakening.

"Shhh…" Arpan said. "Relax and breathe deeply. Relax, and trust me."

Her eyelids began to weigh heavily and she finally couldn't keep them open any more. She felt the needle in her arm before she even noticed that her sleeves had been pulled back. Everything was so out of sync all of a sudden. Despite her drowsiness she didn't drift off to sleep, but heard him talk to her in a monotonous continuous voice. She tried to make out what he was saying but her mind just couldn't take it in. She seemed on some level however to respond to what he said and answer him and have emotional responses to what he told her. It was as if part of her was in another room while she was trying to listen through the door to what was being said. As the conversation 'next door' was going on, she gradually became calmer and more relaxed. She stopped caring about anything and settled into her own cosy feeling. She was content and happy beyond anything she had felt in years. Her entire life seemed to be falling into place, seemed easy to handle and perfectly suited for her.

Then she could hear herself and Arpan calling her into 'the other room'. She thought she saw a door, opened it and walked through it. That was the moment she opened her eyes and realised that she had been sleeping and dreaming all along.

"Welcome back," Anuj said.

"Yes, welcome back," Arpan said as well, smiling deeply and warmly. "Surprised?" he added with a wink.

"No," she said, still dreamy. "Not at all."

"Good!" He got up, squeezed her hand briefly and left the cottage.

"We've got to get you home now," Anuj said. "Your time with us has come to its end."

After only a short period recuperating, he pressured her into getting up and going. In the spot where she had parked her car last time was a little old orange coloured VW Beetle. Anuj got into the driver's seat and Erica got in the back.

Anuj said nothing on the drive to the B&B. He stayed clear of the property and got Erica to walk the last stretch of the road. Mrs Jones was friendly but distant, clearly a little coy, confirming the suspicions in Erica's mind that it was her who had blown the whistle. Uncharacteristically, the woman asked no personal questions and after taking Erica's money made her excuses and busied herself in the kitchen.

Unlike Erica had feared, there were no roadblocks with men in black suits holding machine guns. Anuj drove her unimpeded and quietly to the next train station where Erica got out of the car. She had prepared a speech for the moment and had wanted to say something meaningful as farewell, but she was too dizzy and too tired to remember anything or come up with something new. She stood there like a lemon while Anuj in turn did not stir from his seat and only said a curt: "Look after yourself!"

The train journey was a big blur of noisy teenagers, bouts of nausea, short periods of sleep and a sudden fixation to find out as quickly as possibly what had happened to her cancer. Was she cured now or not? She needed to know.

Part 2

Chapter 12

Erica could hardly remember how she managed to negotiate her way from the train station across London back to her penthouse apartment near Canary Wharf. Once inside she went to bed and slept for what seemed a lifetime. When she awoke it was only to close the curtains or use the bathroom, then she fell asleep again. Not even hunger or thirst could end this sleep marathon.

At long last her exhausted body seemed to have rested sufficiently and she crawled out of her bed, lunchtime, two days after she had arrived back home. It was Sunday now and after a short trip to the local convenience store for food, she spent the rest of the day going through her mail and her financial affairs. She sat on her desk by the window, overlooking the River Thames but her mind was so focused on the paper work that she entirely forgot to take in the spectacular view.

The apartment building had once been a warehouse, cleverly converted by a property developer; it had a receptionist, mail delivery for its residents and had the character of a wonderful luxurious retreat. Her one bedroom flat was very small but it had a fantastic, large balcony and after many years, it still looked brand-new and picture perfect with its modern design and high quality furniture. Now drained of her savings and with an uncertain professional future ahead of her, she might not be able to afford it for much longer and be forced to move. She made calculations of her outgoings and her potential income. She could probably keep her car, whenever it was returned to her but she had no real need for it now that she was back in London. It had been nice to have the option of using her own car once in a while and the garage of the building was a safe place but on her list of possible savings it would be the first item to go.

In her line of work there was no such thing as job security or income guarantee. Her job had been given to someone else who wouldn't have to step down from it again unless management wanted Erica back. She hoped that would be the case but it was far from certain. A few months off were a long time in the business. She might well find herself being pushed down a few steps on the career ladder and having to work her way back up. That could include a pay cut so she had to assume a worst case scenario and see how she could cut her current expenses.

The 12.03% of her money that Arpan had left her would cover her for a little while. She was still on sick leave and would receive 'pay cheques' from her health insurance for a little longer. She thanked her lucky stars that she had never bothered getting on the property ladder. It had helped when she had to declare all of her financial assets to Arpan and it spared her the complications regarding mortgage payments.

Her career was not just dependant on her boss and his goodwill, a lot of it would have to do with luck. The competitive nature in her field of work didn't lend itself to long absences. Once a client became used to dealing with one of Erica's colleagues they might be lost for good, in the same way as she had 'stolen' some of their clients over the years. Her accounts had all been taken over by someone over the last few weeks, someone whom Hilda had thought of as incompetent but maybe that was her loyalty speaking.

Once she had a clean bill of health Erica would have to throw all of her energy into her comeback. She thought she had done enough groundwork with most of her clients to get them running back to her but there were no guarantees.

The calculations for her financial future were promising and seemed doable even in the worst case scenario. Too busy with the paper work she decided not to bother cooking and to treat herself to a take-out instead. Hilda had pushed her into a healthy lifestyle and a special diet that avoided certain foods, believed to aggravate cancer. It was all to do with acidosis; she had a list of approved choices pinned to the fridge door. With enormous pleasure she ripped the piece of paper off and threw it into the bin and ordered a pizza with extra cheese. After her long sleep she felt invincible.

Tomorrow she would go to her doctor and get a new scan. She couldn't wait to find out if Arpan's treatment had been successful. Her mind was still trying to keep up with her week in the Welsh woods and the physical experiences that she had had. Arpan's spell had brought her entire belief system into question. Now that she was back in her flat in London these recent events were starting to feel surreal and unbelievable. What had the elixir done to her? Her body spoke a language of its own and it told her that she was strong and healthy but her mind and rational way of thinking had a few different things to say. During the treatment she had been under a hypnotic and mind-altering spell and continuously on some kind of a high and oblivious to sense and reason. She had agreed to let her car be driven across Britain by a total stranger and was happy to be put on a train back to London, with only her backpack. She had behaved in a manner she had never thought possible and undergone experiences that defied belief.

Removed from that environment, all of it seemed like a hallucination. It was important for Erica to find out as soon as possible what had happened to her body so she could get a grip on reality and a handle on her world again.

Once she had completed her paperwork she enjoyed the guilty pleasures of pizza, wine, trashy TV and the fabulous view from her window. She tried but was unable to get hold of Hilda. Halfway through her stay in Wales her assistant had stopped answering any of her phones, it was quite spooky. When she called the firm she was told that Hilda was on sick leave but the mobile phone was also switched off and there was no reply on her landline either. Erica was beginning to wonder if she should contact the police and hospitals. It was reassuring to find when Erica checked her bank accounts that Hilda had done everything correct and perfectly. Where on earth was the woman now?

Her worries about the mysterious stalkers at the B&B, the interest in her by the drug company and that awful, horse-toothed Julia had subsided the longer she was back here in London and she felt pretty safe again. The apartment building was totally secure and in this big city, Erica was never alone. There were always far too many people around for her to feel threatened and besides, Arpan had led a trail to Scotland by using her car, so she was hopeful that she wasn't on anyone's radar just yet.

She had come up with a battle plan. Once she had obtained an official scan result and knew what the state of her health was, she would make sure said results were stored somewhere safe. Then she would happily meet Julia and agree to their laboratory examinations. As long as there was a certified and official record that the tumour had gone, Julia would be unable to create false records for Erica of her own or do her harm in any way.

It was good to be back in the land of the living and recapturing her life. She had sworn to herself that if she had been given a second chance that she would change, would stop working so hard, make real friends and enjoy her life to the full, but now she felt that she was actually quite content with the way things always had been and that she didn't need or want to change anything.

Her many deeply felt regrets were wiped away and she couldn't wait to get back in the saddle and do as she always had done. She had tried to log into her office email account but in anticipation of her not coming back the IT guys must have changed her password: another thing to do first thing tomorrow morning.

The week had been such a rollercoaster of emotions and so full of hope alternating with doubt and fears; all within the realms of a belief system that defied rational thought. She was amazed however at how certain she felt that she had been cured; this certainty was really the only remnant of the previous seven days.

Her phone vibrated, announcing the arrival of a new email. It was from Julia. There was no way Erica would read that tonight. She switched off her phone and shut down the window with her email provider and indulged herself by watching the rerun of a TV series about a serial killer. At last death didn't concern her anymore and could be entertainment again.

Monday morning she went straight to her doctor who was happy to refer her to a private clinic who could perform an ultrasound scan on her that very day. On her way there she received notifications on her phone about more emails from Julia. Somehow that woman had managed to send her text messages, too. Erica was annoyed that her privacy had been compromised by this horrible woman. Very insistently, the texts had asked Erica to read the emails or contact the sender via the number used for the text.

"Fat chance," Erica whispered under her breath.

She decided to take the underground to the clinic. She couldn't shake the feeling that someone was following her. It was more than a general sense of paranoia; she knew that someone really was following her, even though she couldn't see them. A certainty and sense of knowing that was unlike an unspecific feeling of fear. Twice she thought she had seen someone ducking for cover behind other pedestrian; she probably had given the game away by continuously looking over her shoulder. Luckily the clinic was in the centre of town and located on a busy street, so there was no danger of anybody approaching and threatening her.

The receptionist at the clinic was already expecting her with forms to fill in and within half an hour of reading magazines in the beautiful and expensively furnished waiting room she was led into a small examination room with the all-important scanner.

She was told to strip down to her underwear and wait for Dr Kowalski. An Eastern European woman with thick horn rimmed glasses entered the room shortly after and greeted her briefly in a heavy accent before instructing her to get on the examination table. At first Erica had thought the woman was in her fifties, maybe because of the air of confidence and professionalism that surrounded her, but when she inspected her closer she found the doctor to be much younger. Slim, not an ounce of fat on her, and looking extremely serious.

"It is not my first time," Erica joked as she lay down on the table, but the woman ignored her, seemingly focused entirely on her work.

"What is it you want from this scan?" Dr Kowalski asked, still in a tone that sounded unfriendly. "The notes from your doctor indicate clearly that the tumour is very advanced, and you know that. So why are we looking at it again? Is it a second opinion you want, or do you want to see how fast it grows?"

Under different circumstances Erica would have risen to these suggestive comments but her mind was too focused on the outcome.

"I don't think it is there anymore," Erica said excitedly. "Please just do the scan," she added, now also abruptly, since the woman shook her head in a rude gesture of undisguised disagreement and ridicule.

"Propána," the doctor whispered and breathed heavily. She began with the scan but soon she was looking flustered and confused. "Jesus," she seemed to whisper under her breath, hardly loud enough to be heard.

"Wait a moment," she said to Erica as composed as she could muster and she stormed out of the room. When she came back she had two more doctors with her and the three alternated trying to locate Erica's tumour. Each one took a turn at operating the scanner and shook their head, all without a single word being said.

"Come to the other examination room," her original doctor said. She gave Erica a dressing gown and led her across the hallway. The second scanner produced the same results, it seemed. "Neuvěřitelný!" Dr Kowalksi said at last.

"We need to do more tests," one of her colleagues said. "We must do an X-ray."

This was done immediately and also carried out in the same building. Afterwards Erica was left again with just the magazines in the waiting room for company.

Shortly after noon the receptionist appeared and asked Erica to come into the doctor's office, where the other two doctors soon joined them.

"It's unbelievable! Mrs Miller, there must have been some mix up in your records. Maybe because of your recent name change, no? In any case, you need to take this up with an industry watchdog. Your doctors or their administrators have done you a great disservice," she ranted loudly.

"This was not even done by the NHS," she whispered to her colleagues. "An outrage!"

One of them spoke to her quickly in that other language and a heated debate took place between the two of them.

"What are you planning to do?" the third doctor asked Erica.

"Nothing," she replied. "All I care about are these results. I will not take this any further, an honest mistake seems to have been made. There is nothing to be gained from pointing fingers and suing people. I'm happy and lucky to be alive."

"Mrs Miller, you are certainly lucky," Dr Kowalski said. "It's fortunate that you didn't jump off a bridge or sold your house and spent all of your money," she added. "A medical blunder like this needs to be accounted for so that it will not happen again. You have a responsibility to take this up with the authorities."

119

"Thank you, but all I want to do after my ordeal is to get back to my life and forget this ever happened."

"Very well," Dr Kowalski said. "You need to do as you need to do."

The receptionist gave her a copy of the astronomical bill, for which she had already paid a deposit with her credit card; a huge dent into her restricted budget. Thank heavens for the 12.03% that Arpan kindly had left her. Erica went straight to her solicitor and had the documents which accompanied her scan results, copied, verified and held with the solicitor.

Unsure if someone was still following her or not, she went to the nearest post office and sent sealed copies of these documents to a bunch of trusted people for safe keeping. Her shadow might know which clinic and solicitor she had gone to, but they couldn't know to whom she had sent the documents to. Now that she had succeeded in securing the preservation of those documents she finally felt perfectly safe and was happy to meet her stalker or Julia herself if needed.

Before she was going to respond to the woman's email, Erica decided to go to her workplace and speak to them about her future career prospects, so she could get that out of the way.

With the evidence of her healing being successfully in the bag, as it were, she decided to treat herself to a taxi. She was healthy and would be able to earn a decent salary for the foreseeable future. Even if she would have to go down a few levels in the hierarchy first.

Her boss Mike was surprised when she phoned him and asked for an audience with him. Mike was a big headed guy but he had always had a soft spot for Erica, if for no other reasons than that she was always coming out with the guys and never gave him grief about his borderline racist or sexist jokes. It was a fantastic feeling to enter the halls of her firm again. The buildings in Canary Wharf had magnificence about them. Swiping her identity card at the security gates she walked confidently past the receptionists' desk – it was like being back home, at last. It was almost more familiar than her flat, where she usually was on her own. Here she was used to interacting with people and knew the rules of engagement.

She took the elevator to the seventh floor and walked through the corridors towards Mike's office. The people here of course still thought she was going to die of cancer, so they avoided her and either pretended that they had not seen her, or they smiled awkwardly towards her and moved on.

Mike was a well groomed, handsome man in his early forties, who reminded people of the man from a famous cigarette advert. He had a lot of active energy and got out of his chair the second he saw her through the glass walls of his office.

"You're looking well," he said jokingly as he enthusiastically shook her hand. "Are you here to get your job back?" he asked and laughed out loud.

She smiled and offered him her hand. It was a private joke between them that he would kiss her hand like a gentleman, only to pinch her behind a second later, to which she would reply: "Oh beehive." He didn't take the bait because she had not played the game with him since her fatal diagnosis. He gestured her to have a seat and sat down opposite her in his large leathery seat.

"Guess what: I am!" she said full of excitement. "I've taken a turn for the better."

He laughed a little too uncomfortably. "Good one, Erica. We could really do with you onboard right now, actually. I landed us a fantastic new account this morning. It's with a massive pharmaceutical company from Europe. I'll ask them to find a cure for your cancer, shall I?"

Again he roared at his own joke and smiled at her for joining in.

"Well, seriously now," he said and addressed her in a jovial and helpful manner, "what can I do you for? Do you need help with an insurance claim or something?"

"No, I've got it all covered," she replied and looked directly at him, serious. "I really am fit to work. I have a doctor's note that says so and I would very much like to resume my old position if I may."

Mike looked at her worriedly. "Are you alright, love? Are you on drugs or something?"

"I'm not, of course, or else I would have offered them to you right away, wouldn't I?" she said drily. "Listen, I have some documents here that show that the tumour is no more. Or most likely, that it never was. They must have mixed up my files with someone else's. Look," she said and opened her handbag with the envelopes. "I had a scan and X-ray this morning."

121

"Erica, what can I say?" he stuttered after he had quickly scanned the letter from the clinic. "You said you wouldn't come back here. We did you a favour by keeping you on the payroll but that was only to stop you from having to go on benefits. We didn't expect you to come back. We have filled your position already." He seemed very uncomfortable for such a confident man.

"I'm not stupid, Mike," she said calmly. "I know that, and I certainly appreciate what you did for me. I'm not coming here as some militant union freak to make ridiculous demands. You know me better than that. I can look after myself alright, but you know that I'm damn good at my job and you would be an idiot to let me go. There must be something else somewhere in the firm, even on a lower rank, so I can go back and work my way up to the top again."

Mike looked uncomfortably to the corridor. The phone rang and he answered it. He listened for a minute or two, then he said "I understand, of course, thank you," and hung up.

He breathed another heavy sigh as his expression turned from uncomfortable to anger.

"You have some nerve," he said suddenly.

"What do you mean?" She asked surprised at the change of tone. What was the matter with him?

He sighed deeply, then stood up and paced around the room, not looking at her as he was speaking.

"I like you, Erica, and I wish you well. I always have. But you know goddamn well how competitive our industry is."

"Yes, and I never let you down in my entire career here." She pointed out with pride in her voice.

"We told your clients why you left the firm," he confessed sheepishly.

"You did what?" she almost screamed. "How dare you?"

"We didn't have a choice in the matter," Mike defended himself. "Some of your clients wanted you back so badly, they refused to be helped by any of our other agents, so eventually we leaked the information, so we could get them off our back and hook them up with our other agents who, honestly, could do the work just as well as you."

"That's professional assassination," Erica said fuming.

"It was or is the goddamn truth for crying out loud and we needed to make sure they wouldn't go to other agencies. How were we to know you would wander back in here and come up with this story."

"I don't believe this," she said. "I'm dead in this town. No other agency will have me."

"Well, you can't go round telling people you have cancer and then be surprised that they freak when you suddenly come back and claim it was a mistake. I think you're better off trying to find out who switched your medical results; hire yourself an awesome lawyer and sue them for the last sorry penny that they have."

"Holy fuck!" she uttered.

"For what it's worth: you were quite a hit and maybe a few of your old customers might feel charitable enough to hire you back. Maybe we can figure something out so you can work on a freelance basis on their accounts but the majority of the customers won't touch you now. Nobody wants to be reminded of death and cancer. We're a happy firm and our clients come here because we laugh and smile and make them feel good."

"Nobody in London will ever give me a job, thanks to your indiscretion," she said fuming. "Once you're linked with cancer, you're always remembered for it. How could you? You got me into this mess, you will have to sort it out, or I will sue you!" she threatened. "Speak to Human Resources and say you made a mistake. Then ring the clients and tell them that I'm back and that the cancer diagnosis was a clerical error."

"Who do you think will buy that story? I was kind enough to read your little letter here, but let's face it. One of two documents has to be a fake. Either the initial diagnose, which makes me wonder where you spent the time while not being at work, maybe in the Bahamas or Tahiti, or the new one is fake, which renders you unfit for work and nothing has changed."

"Don't be absurd, Mike. You know me. I'm a workaholic. I have weeks of saved up leave that I never used. I would never skive a single day."

"As I said: Human Resources would never stand for it. Who are they to believe? The old or the new certificate? One of them is fake, and to be brutally honest, my money is on the new one. You miss the office and your sense of purpose. You said so yourself: you're a workaholic. I wish I could help you and find you something to do to make your situation more bearable, but we're not a charity and we can't take a chance on you, only to find out that the cancer suddenly has made a re-appearance. Don't do this to me! You know I'd do anything I could possibly do for you."

"So what do you suggest?" she asked, close to tears. She had never anticipated so much resistance.

"If you need to do something, do some charity work. Spend time with your family. Just don't come here anymore. Please hand me over your pass to the building."

This was her worst nightmare come true. She had thought that her life was finally back on track when it had unravelled into pieces once again.

Without resistance she handed him the lanyard with her ID and got up.

"Call reception to let me out," she said. "Tell Hilda to call me when she's back. I need to speak to her."

"If you…" Mike started but she interrupted him.

"Don't worry. Not about that. I need to speak to her about something private. I won't try anything funny and compromise her position, too. She's been a damn good friend to me while I was ill. Thanks Mike and good luck with your life."

"Same to you, love. Look after yourself."

On her way out she bumped into Helen, one of her former drinking partners and rival to several accounts over the years. Despite their many differences, Helen seemed to have at least temporarily forgotten that Erica was on sick leave and greeted her with the usual fake smile and friendliness.

"We really need more staff now that we have the pharmaceutical account opening," she said. "It's a huge firm, I cannot believe Mike managed to land them. The man is a magician. We will definitely need more agents," she added. Then she suddenly seemed to remember the cancer and looked bedazzled and embarrassed.

"Oh, my God! I am so sorry," Helen said, covering her mouth with her hands. "I completely forgot. How are you these days?" She looked Erica up and down and shook her head: "You are looking damn well," she said before Erica could reply.

Erica smiled triumphantly but stopped herself in time before blurting out about her healing. She was just trying to formulate a reply when she saw Julia from the dreaded drug company walking into Mike's office. Now she got it. That was the account everyone was talking about. Erica quickly ducked behind Helen to make sure the woman didn't see her.

"What's the matter?" Helen asked concerned.

"Oh, I just had a dizzy spell," Erica lied unconvincingly. "Who is that woman?"

"That is the new big client," Helen replied. "Very scary, isn't she? I hate women executives, they always seem to be extra mean to over compensate, don't they?"

"You and I are women executives, you dork!" Erica replied and then walked towards the elevator.

"Call me!" Helen said, almost as if she meant it.

Erica could feel the world closing in on her. She rushed back to her flat to think about her next move. When she got to her building the receptionist stopped her.

"Mrs Whittaker, have you got a minute?"

Erica looked with suspicion at Martin, the man who had buzzed her into the building for years. Grossly overweight from all the sitting, in his late twenties and normally always cheerful he had become almost a friend to her but his look today did not look promising.

"Sure, what's up?" she asked.

"I'm afraid I have bad news," he said, and handed her an envelope. "Your landlord has decided to end your contract. You'll have to move out of here. I shall miss you."

Erica grabbed the envelope from him and without saying a word she took it with her to her penthouse. When she opened the letter she saw that it was true. It was an official notice, not giving any reason. Not that they had to but it seemed odd, since the owner was an investment group in Switzerland, who had no reason to single her out like this. Unless… of course... it could be no coincidence that Erica had effectively been sacked this morning, the same day as Mike had landed that account with the firm. Now this.

It was time to meet the devil and negotiate.

Erica switched on her laptop and opened her email, found Julia's message and replied:

Let's meet.

A minute after sending it her mobile phone sprang into action.

"I'm glad you're finally making time for a little chat," she heard the acerbic voice. "I'm on my way over to your building as we speak. I'll be with you very shortly. We have a lot to talk about."

There was hardly any time for Erica to prepare for the upcoming confrontation. Well, never mind, she prepped herself, she would wing it somehow.

"What a cosy little place," Julia said after she was let into the apartment. "You shall miss it dearly, I'd expect. Pity these rental contracts. You get used to living somewhere and then someone decides you have to move out. I prefer owning."

"I saw you at the agency with Mike and it can't be a coincidence that I was sacked by him the very same day that I lose the apartment. I take it you are behind all of this?"

Julia looked at her almost bored without either confirming or denying anything.

"Why don't you save yourself the gloating and the venom and tell me what you have come here for. I'm sure we both can make better use of our time than beating around the bush."

"Fine," Julia said with a smirk. "Let me come straight to the point; you lost our job, your friends and your apartment but you recently got your health back I understand and with it your life. You can hardly complain about the deal. Professionally, as far as advertising work in London is concerned, you're history. At least it will be a steep uphill struggle to control the awful damage that has been done to your reputation. Maybe you can cash in on a book deal about Arpan and the miracle elixir, but chances are, nobody will believe you and you'll be entirely discredited."

"You're still gloating. You must have something else to tell me," Erica said, trying to calm her anger. "Why else would you be here – personally."

"Oh yes," Julia said. "I do have more to say. What good would it do me to see you struggle and having to keep an eye on you all of the time. I'm much more practical than that. So now that your career has come to an abrupt end and you'll be forced to leave your apartment, I'm offering you a new life. I know what Arpan has done and you were clever enough to get proof of it

126

before we got to you. Well played, my dear. I take it that you sent the certified copies of the original to several places, making it next to impossible for us to retrieve them."

"Spot on," Erica said smugly.

"Well, maybe you think of me more of a monster than I actually am. The easiest way to handle this is to make you dependent on us, with positive results for all of us. We'll hire you and we'll find you a new life outside of London and the UK. You're an intelligent woman, and unofficially Mike has given me the most glowing reference for you. Where would you like to work? New York? Zurich? Munich? Lausanne?"

"I'll have to think about that," Erica said.

"You can think about the location, but I need an answer and a signature from you right now," Julia said impatiently. "You've taken up far too much of my time already and if you're unwilling to cooperate we will need to think of something else to do with you entirely."

"I'll sign if you can guarantee that Arpan will not come to any harm and that you will continue the work you're doing for him. He's been so wonderfully kind towards me, I really don't want him to suffer because of it."

"I know he's a real saint and boo hoo, but if I don't take some kind of punitive measures in retaliation then I'm sending him mixed messages, and that would certainly not be fair on him either."

"What are you going to do?" Erica asked, welling up with regret and guilt.

"Oh don't be so melodramatic Erica. I thought you'd be more professional than that. At least that's what Mike had promised me about you. Tut tut. Of course he won't come to harm and we will continue our end of the bargain with him," Julia replied, rather convincingly. "We went through a lot of red tape to set all of this orphanage business up, we got a lot of kudos for it and we would be silly to abandon it now. We try to keep Arpan on our side; there is no need to punish him. We scared him a little, that should do the trick. As long as we're keeping up that orphanage he is as happy as Larry. It's an easy deal."

"What kind of position did you have in mind for me?" Erica asked.

"Your CV is pretty impressive, and so is your reputation. It depends where you want to work as I'm sure we can find you something that suits you almost anywhere: marketing, advertising, PR. Mind you, we'd have to figure out if you have gone all moral on us now since you've had your life altering experience with Arpan," she said.

"What do you mean?" Erica asked.

"I mean, can you sell our more controversial or rather, our heavily criticised activities to the press and politicians? Can you see things our way? It requires a certain mature approach to what we do: a wider perspective and pragmatism. If you have gone all soft because of your contact with Arpan, we may have to find you something more clerical instead."

Erica hesitated.

"Not to worry, it will be worth your while financially," Julia said with an impatient roll of her eyes.

"I wish I knew exactly how controversial your policies are," Erica said.

"Clerical it is," Julia said snappy. "If you even have to think about it, I guess you won't have what it takes. I would recommend our Munich office. The new building is in a wonderful location; judging from your current river view penthouse, it seems as if that is important to you. The new site in Bavaria is in a great spot. We have an office in the inner city if you prefer the buzz, but the main site is outside of town and it has some stunning views of the mountains. Say the word and we will get you moved down there within a week."

Chapter 13

Erica loved her new life; Julia had unpleasant characteristics, but she was no liar. Her new position at the Munich branch of the company was clerical, not very demanding; it left plenty of time to do anything she liked during working hours and stare dreamily at the mighty, snow covered mountains across the border in Austria from her office. Since she had been handpicked for the position, she didn't feel the competitive pressure that had been so predominant in her previous work environments. Her colleagues here were friendly and had no hidden agendas whatsoever. It seemed that the office was one big family that looked out for each other. They took her out in the evenings when she first arrived to help her settle in. All her colleagues spoke English fluently and came from all over the world. The scientists and the administrators all gelled as if they were all on the same level; there was no sense of hierarchy or separation. For Erica it was just too good to be true. She began evening classes to learn German where she met Gunnar, a Swedish lab assistant whom she started dating. She was swayed by his earthy mannerisms and his simple attitude towards life; he grasped every minute of his life and she was happy to join in.

Gunnar was a few years younger than her and incredibly handsome. Nothing seemed too much effort for him, he was a breath of fresh air. He got her to go to the company gym with him and take up some of the many activities that Bavaria lent itself to: cycling, kayaking and hiking in the nearby mountains. Despite his many outdoor interests, when he first arrived he opted for a little flat in the centre of Munich and now that had the added benefit that Erica had the best of both worlds – country living and city action, whenever she wanted.

Her body was in better shape than it ever had been, she was surprised to find that even though she had never bothered training it, now, past 40, she was capable of getting it into such good shape, defying gravity and the downward trend that her friends of similar age always had moaned about. She occasionally thought that it might have had to do with Arpan and his healing but soon dismissed such thoughts. The entire episode seemed in the long and distant past. Two years had passed and her thoughts on the matter were beginning to change. Being in a scientific, environment surrounded by rational, albeit in certain aspects narrow minded, thinkers was beginning to rub off on her. Without a Hilda or an Aunt Bethany to back up discussions about alternative therapies, she would have felt completely unable explaining her experience to anyone here without sounding unconvincing, even to herself.

Julia had assured her that Arpan was fine and Erica had no reason to doubt her. The orphanage that Arpan had been so adamant about keeping was a big publicity project for the company and was not only frequently covered in the in-house publication but in national magazines, too; shutting it down would never have been an option and Erica wondered if Arpan was aware of that.

However, Erica paid little attention to it all, she was swept away by the many new opportunities and grateful for the way her life had been rescued and turned around. The only thing she regretted was that she never had heard from Hilda again. Part of her agreement with Julia had strangely included that she were not to contact anyone who knew of her cancer scare; that suited her fine but the only person she missed was her former assistant. Given the speed with which the move to Germany had happened, Erica wouldn't have been able to find the time to track Hilda down anyway. She knew that her assistant – like Erica - had never returned to work in the advertising company. Hilda was probably on Julia's payroll in the Lausanne or New York office.

Her new relationship with Gunnar soon took over all of Erica's life. He was passionate and made great demands on her time and he took her to meet his family and friends in Uppsala in Sweden – much earlier than what dating etiquette dictated. From day one he was planning joint holidays with her abroad.

"We could take the night train from Munich to Rome," he would say. "Spend the day there and take the morning train back home. It'd be the perfect short weekend getaway. I can't believe you've never been to Rome. Or how about a flight to Budapest? You need to lose your island mentality and realise how close everything is in Europe."

When she had worked in the advertising business she had pulled all-nighters and never got round to mini breaks. Even when she planned to see people and booked a long weekend somewhere, usually she had to cancel last minute because of a deadline or a creative block that left her work in limbo. She was amazed that the world was her oyster now and she couldn't think of a single reason to be cautious and say no to Gunnar's many plans.

"Okay, let's do it," she said and felt ecstatic over the new ease of her life.

"If you like train journeys, we should do the Trans-Siberian Railway together," Gunnar suggested dreamily, excited by the thought. "We could even fly to Hawaii once we are that far east."

She was sucked in by his whirlwind of energy just as he was taken by her newly found appreciation of life and its unlimited possibilities. The only thing she disliked about him was his love of Scandinavian hard-rock music. He tortured her with this his insatiable appetite for it. He was most upset when she declined to go to a concert of one of his favourite bands; eventually she gave in to his sulking and accompanied him. All the while she was scared and a little suspicious of what she saw as a wild and untamed side to him that she hadn't seen before.

She never told him about her experience with Arpan. It seemed too much to tell anyone who hadn't known her before and particularly inappropriate to mention it to someone so down to earth and worldly as Gunnar. From time to time it had occurred to her to bring it up and she waited for an opportune moment, but after two years in Munich it seemed no longer possible for her to relate to the experiences. Even though she had still some very clear recollections and medical records to prove it, she thought it unwise to risk her happy relationship by introducing something so obscure from her past that could happily stay there. Since she was dating someone from the company and she had signed the non-disclosure contract, she had really no choice than not to tell him anyway. If Julia ever got wind of it, it would be a disaster.

"Let's go to Prague this weekend," Gunnar said one night. "I have some points on my hotel loyalty card and we seem to only ever travel south to Austria or Italy."

"Yes, why not," she said, once more amazed at his continuous bouts of energy.

A short plane ride took them to the beautiful city with its well preserved and maintained historic buildings, the famous

Charles Bridge over the river and the castle towering above the city.

"It's very touristy," Erica said as they strolled through the pedestrianized city centre. "It's almost too beautiful and too good to be true."

"I thought you'd find it romantic," he said taken aback.

"You bringing me here is very romantic," she said, quickly backtracking. She had noticed a little nervousness about him and she had come to half expect him to propose to her on this trip. Some of his Nordic, reserved manners remained and often he didn't give much away about the way he felt: he only had a few tells. Despite their age difference, he seemed undeterred and very keen on her. On the other hand she couldn't forget the tough rocker that came out when he was listening to that awful music.

A bit of a geek, as many of her new friends were, Gunnar clumsily bought her a glass heart instead of the more artistic artefacts on offer at the many stalls spread all over the city centre. He had booked one of the most expensive hotels in Prague with his loyalty points and was disappointed when he saw that the room was not the one he had seen advertised online.

"It's still a great hotel and a fantastic location," she had consoled him. "What did you expect for your points? They cannot give you such luxury for free. They tried to get you through the door cheaply so that you get a taste for the real thing. It's free, that's all that matters."

"I know. I should have expected this but I had a different vision of our holiday."

When she took a shower he rang the concierge and arranged for a table at a recommended restaurant. They took a stroll along the river before getting into a stunningly ornamented, traditional looking restaurant, located in a very well preserved historical stone building. Gunnar took her confidently past the queue outside and had them escorted to a cosy table in a corner of the more rustic basement room of the restaurant. Low ceilings with wooden décor gave a very authentic and atmospheric historical ambience. The prices were very steep and it was obvious to her that this was meant to be a compensation for the regular hotel room that had disappointed Gunnar so much.

Erica looked through the menu when she suddenly felt a sharp pain radiating from her back. It was the same type of stomach and back pain that had turned out to be the first signs of her cancer. Panic immediately consumed her. She quickly excused herself and got up to go to the ladies to have a moment to think about this in quiet but Gunnar was too wrapped up in the delights of the menu to think much of it. She reached the safety of a cubicle and began to feel her back and stomach. No, it couldn't be, she thought. It couldn't have come back. She pulled herself together and re-did her makeup in the mirror.

Despite expectations to the contrary, Gunnar didn't propose that evening but he was in a very amorous mood and paid her plenty of compliments. Erica was pre-occupied and a little distant, maybe that put him off. She was deeply unsettled, especially since the painkillers she had taken didn't seem to make much difference. The food tasted delicious but she couldn't really appreciate it. Gunnar took her back to the hotel, visibly disappointed at her lack of enthusiasm.

She turned down his advances in the bedroom and asked him to organise some stronger pain killers, implying she had woman's problems.

"You're not due those for another week," he pointed out. She was shocked to find out he knew. Her past boyfriends would never have known about that. She smiled at the many ways she thought he was a typical Swede.

"Please, just get me some painkillers all the same. I'm sure the concierge must be able to help."

Gunnar left the room to fulfil the mission while she tried to calm herself, but to no avail. She was consumed by naked fear.

Gunnar eventually came back empty handed. The concierge had not been able or willing to help him and had given Gunnar the impression he was insulted for being treated like a black market drug dealer.

"He was holding a speech about how we tourists seem to think we can bypass the laws by throwing money at them. He was very touchy about it," he reported back. "Maybe we should call out a doctor?"

"No," she said. "I will be fine."

He ordered her a hot water bottle and gave her some sleeping tablets he had in his travel kit; they knocked her out until the next morning. The pain was still there, although a little less prominent. She had a dizzy spell in the shower and almost fell but managed to sit down on the floor before she blanked out and collapsed.

Gunnar was alarmed and panicked when he found her. He was about to call for an ambulance when Erica came to and stopped him. She insisted she was fine.

"You're not pregnant, are you?" he asked. The look he gave her didn't reveal if that were desirable a surprise for him or not.

"Certainly not," she said, making her feelings on the matter clearly known.

Since she could stand up and move about the room, Gunnar let the idea of an ambulance or doctor slide.

"It's probably a side effect of the sleeping tablet," she insisted. "We should tell the company about it."

The joke silenced him and gave her an opportunity to come to a decision about what to do about her pain. The normal thing would be to go back to Munich and have her doctor check her out, maybe even ask Julia for the use of the in-house facilities, but then she thought also of Arpan and the repercussions any of her actions might have on him. She didn't want to play into anyone's hands, especially if the pain she had experienced was nothing to do with her cancer, which in any case was clearly the most likely scenario here. She would have preferred to keep everything under wraps until she knew more about it. She owed that much to Arpan.

"You scared me," Gunnar said to her during breakfast in the hotel restaurant. "Maybe you should go to a hospital, just in case. You don't seem yourself today. We should have you checked out."

"It's nothing really," she said quickly.

"It doesn't look as if it is nothing," he insisted. "Let's get you to a hospital to find out."

"We'll do it when I'm back in Munich," she said. "There's no point in spoiling what is left of our mini-break."

"We can always come back here. Something's wrong with you and I won't waste a single day to get to the bottom of this."

"Maybe," she said hesitatingly. "But if I do, I want to go to a private clinic."

"The state hospitals here are pretty good," Gunnar pointed out. "Eastern Europe has never been primitive in its health care," he added.

She looked at Gunnar and wondered what to make of him. She had decided to accept his proposal when it came, so she should really think of him as her partner, but with his rational side she was unsure if she could tell him about Arpan, the cancer and the deal with Julia. He was also an employee at the company where the terms and conditions of her contract prohibited discussing this part of her past with any of her colleagues. Telling him was in breach of the agreement and could terminate her work there immediately.

"You must not breathe a word about this to anyone, do you understand me? I hope you haven't texted anyone, have you?" she asked concerned.

"Of course not," he said, clearly confused by her seriousness. "Why are you so funny about this?"

"You must swear not to tell anyone what I'm about to tell you now, can you do that?" she asked him.

"Of course I can do that, sweetheart. What's eating you? Tell me all about it, I'm here for you," he reassured her and clumsily grabbed her hand.

She played nervously with her watch and gathered all of her courage for this leap of faith.

"Three years ago, I was diagnosed with terminal pancreatic cancer. It was already stage four. It had spread everywhere and I was waiting to die," she said.

"Impossible," he said, "you know that's impossible. You wouldn't be here if that were true."

"I know how this must sound to you," she said. "Please hear me out. I'm as rational a person as you are."

He stared at her with a coldness she'd never seen. Undeterred she carried on.

"I know it's unbelievable but I went to a famous healer and he made the cancer go away."

"No way," Gunnar said, shaking his head. "Don't be absurd."

"You must trust me," she begged him. "It's true. I know it's hard to swallow but that's exactly what happened to me."

"I can't believe you would tell me such nonsense," he said and got up from the table. "I know people who make up stories like this for attention, but I never had you down as one of them."

He threw the napkin on the table and stormed off without a further word or a look back at her.

Erica was shocked at his violent response. She had thought of many possible responses but 'attention seeking' had never crossed her mind.

She finished her breakfast, slightly embarrassed by the scene Gunnar had created, then she went back to their room. He was watching the BBC News Channel when she came in and at first didn't even bother greeting her.

"How could you just leave me like that?" she said accusingly.

"Oh, it is my manners that are off?" he said angrily. "How could you make up some stupid story like the one you just did? What are you trying to achieve with bullshit like that? I love you Erica but I won't stand for you making up ridiculous stories to make yourself important. If you had cancer then it could have only been a stage one or you wouldn't be here. I haven't seen any scars on your body either. So what the hell are you playing at?"

"I understand that this is a lot to take in but you know me better than to think I would make something like this up. I don't need any attention from anyone. Back in Munich I have all the documentation to prove it to you. You can go online and google pancreatic cancer and the name Arpan. See for yourself what people have to say about him. He was mostly active over 20 years ago and he healed many people. He found this elixir that cured pancreatic cancer in combination with his healing abilities."

"It's one thing to go to a fortune teller for a laugh and have them read your palm, Erica, I'm all for a little bit of fun, but going round making far-fetched claims of miracle healings is where I draw the line."

"If I hadn't been so desperate at the time I would never have tried it, but I had nothing to lose. He doesn't practice anymore because Julia paid him off, but he made an exception for me and it worked. Until now, that is. I need to have it checked out, but we have to do it discreetly."

Gunnar stayed away from her, looking at her with disappointment and anger.

"Is this 'Arpan' from a different planet or has he been abducted by aliens? Erica, you're making it worse. You don't need any fantasy stories to be interesting. What has gotten into you all of a sudden?"

"Gunnar, you must believe me," she pleaded.

"To think you know someone after two years and then find out they're completely mad and full of conspiracy theories and delusions," he said. "You have some nerve."

She froze from his icy demeanour.

"You were always too good to be true," he continued. "I really should have known better. Chicks always have a screw loose, you just need to find it before it finds you."

"Go on the internet and check him out," she insisted. "My story is not unique."

"Of course you're not alone. There are plenty of crazies out there. I don't need to check the web. Erica, we've been together for almost two years. If you really had cancer, you would have told me about that by now. How stupid do you think I am?" he asked her. He picked up his wallet and made for the door. "What's the matter with you?"

"You're free to think as you please, but as my boyfriend you owe me to look at the webpages before you dismiss it all," she said desperately.

"Okay then," he said and reluctantly sat down.

Erica grabbed her laptop and went on the net to google Arpan.

"Here look," she said and pointed at the screen.

Gunnar got up and scanned the webpages.

"Yes," he said. "That doesn't prove anything. Plenty of people say the same thing. Where is the scientific explanation, the clinical trials and the patent for his cure?"

"Look at the articles. He has healed hundreds of people," she said. "There must be something about that number that speaks for itself."

"You know me better than to think that I would believe something like this," Gunnar said coldly. "I don't know how he managed to manipulate medical records on such a scale but I don't believe in his *magic* for one minute. If you really had cancer and the *disappearance* of it had anything to with him at all, then it was a freak placebo effect but even that seems really too idiotic. I'm so disappointed in you. To think I was going to ask you to marry me," he said. "What does a man have to do to find a normal woman?"

"Please, Gunnar," she said, tears welling up in her eyes.

"I'd love to believe you, but if you want me to believe in fairy tales then you chose the wrong man."

"I have documents in my flat that can prove it," she said, desperate to get through to him.

"I bet you have," he said. "How sad it has to end like this. I'm out of here."

He began to pack his things.

"We can sort this out in the morning," she tried to keep him back. "I would have said yes."

"Sure you would have. Sorry Erica, I'm done here. I'll take a room of my own. I hate nothing more than liars and attention seekers. I've done it once, and I won't go through it again."

"Wait," she said as he was about to leave. "If this is it between us, you must promise me one thing."

"And what would that be? Ride home on your unicorn?"

"Please don't mention this to anyone at the firm, whatever happens. Nobody must find out about this. You're the only person I've told."

"You got it," he said coolly. "I don't want anyone to think I've been going out with a lunatic, anyway."

"I mean it."

"So do I," he said and with that he left.

Erica wanted to cry but for the time being, her worry about the cancer overrode everything else. She called reception and got the concierge to find her a private health clinic that would see clients on a Sunday. She called the number and to her surprise got an emergency appointment later in the day. Apparently, money could still buy you a lot over here. The taxi ride took her to what appeared to be a predominantly residential quarter of town. Lots of new buildings, painted neatly to fit in with the traditional, ancient look of the rest of the city. The building that housed the clinic had wonderful décor on the outside. Fresh white paint, dark wooden windows that had been tactfully modernised and discreetly double glazed gave the impression of an old residential apartment block. The clinic occupied the entire ground floor. The receptionist, a pretty and eager woman in her thirties named Gabriele, got Erica to fill in some forms –

professionally translated into English - and took her credit card details.

"All I want is for you to scan my pancreas," Erica told Gabriele when she handed her back the completed forms. "I'm pretty sure I know what's going on with me," she added.

Gabriele didn't raise as much as an eye brow and took the forms off her hands with a clinical smile.

An hour later Erica was met by the on-duty doctor, F. Adameck. He was a very confident and relaxed man, in his late twenties, she guessed, who spoke English with a thick Australian accent.

"That is an unusual request," he stated when she had declared her situation. "You must be the first person ever to walk into a doctor's office to suspect something as specific as pancreatic cancer from stomach and back pain. There are a lot of other tests I would suggest we run to get clues about your symptoms first; it could be kidney stones or many other things."

"I came to a private clinic specifically to avoid all the other crap," she said. "I know it sounds odd but you have to trust me on this one. Please humour me and do the scan."

"I wish it were so simple," the doctor said. "Pancreatic cancer can be visible on ultrasound, but there are times when it is ineffective. For example, you have eaten a big breakfast. In slim patients like yourself overlying bowel gas could obscure the view of the pancreas. I would suggest we take some blood to see if there are any tumour markers, although that won't give us a definite answer about your pancreas, only about the possibility of cancer in your body full stop."

"Please just do the ultrasound and see if that shows any results. Please!"

"We'll start with the blood test and I guess it can't hurt to do an ultrasound test, too, if you are that keen," he said. "It will give us an idea if this is at all likely or possible, but not necessarily an answer. Please bear that in mind in any case."

Dr Adameck instructed Gabriele in Czech through the intercom and then he left the room. Gabriele took Erica's blood and then asked her to come with her to a different treatment room. Half an hour later Dr Adameck appeared and began to operate the ultra sound scanner. He looked bedazzled at the monitor.

"I can't say for sure that this is a tumour," he said carefully. "Your blood shows some tumour markers but they could theoretically come from a different source and be the result of a different disease altogether. They are far from fool-proof. I can certainly see something odd on your pancreas, not unlike a tumour might look, but we need to run more tests," he said.

"Damn it," Erica swore.

"May I ask what made you suspect this? How did you know? I mean, even if your parents had pancreatic cancer this would still be a long shot. There is no strong genetic link for pancreatic cancer," he added. "That is incredible!"

"Call it a hunch," Erica whispered, devastated by the diagnosis.

"The good news is that the tumour is small enough to be surgically removed," he said. "There are of course more factors to consider before we can definitely go ahead with such an operation. From what I can tell it's early stage but we need to get you into an MRI scanner to find out exactly where it is and whether it has affected blood vessels or other surrounding areas. It's highly unusual for you to have any symptoms at all at this stage, which is why I'm a little confused about this. I'm flabbergasted by your intuition. The bad news is, that I don't have an MRI scanner available here and that we would need a specialist for this kind of operation and they tend to be busy."

"It must be done in secret, though. Is there any way to keep this out of official records?" she asked panicking.

"I don't understand you," Dr Adameck said. "You make very odd requests."

"Could you treat me under a different name, so as to keep this quiet?

"If you pay the right kind of money, I'm sure that can be arranged."

After a few phone calls Dr Adameck got her to a larger hospital in Prague that did perform the MRI scan for her two days later. Erica called in sick, half expecting Julia or her minions to come and investigate but they didn't seem concerned. She had not given a specific reason for her absence and could only pray that Gunnar would keep the story to himself and that she could come up with a good cover story once she was back in Munich.

With the results of her scan she was sent to a clinic in the Ukraine where a specialist surgeon was available to remove the tumour.

Erica was shocked to hear about all the risks that were involved in the surgery and the impact this might have on her future life and its quality. Since her previous tumour had been unsuitable for operation due to its size alone, she had never learned more about it. Now she found out that there was another nasty dimension to this volatile disease.

She signed all the waiver forms and hoped for the best. There were no real alternatives except seeing Arpan, but now that her cancer had been found at a stage where she had a choice between western medicine and Arpan's healing, she didn't have to think twice about it. The solution from western medicine was the avenue she would always explore first.

After all, Arpan had claimed that her treatment was efficient for the rest of her life. Anuj had said that she was now immune to cancer. If they had been wrong about this, then Erica had no choice but to throw her trust into the more traditional methods of cancer treatment.

While she endured the preparations for her surgery, she thought a lot about coming clean to Julia about her situation but Erica had a deep distrust of the woman. This would be the perfect opportunity for someone like Julia to take out an enemy. Julia would have proof of Erica's cancer, which meant she could discredit Arpan and his methods publicly. But that was not what she was afraid of. The upcoming operation was a complicated one that entailed many risks. An accident could happen easily and nobody would ask many questions about it. If Julia got wind of her operation there was no guarantee that an accident might not be 'manufactured' to silence an inconvenient person once and for all and without any effort.

The operation in Kiev went well and fortunately without complications. The doctors there even joked about it with Erica, saying that hers was one of the easiest and luckiest tumours they had come across so far. Due to the tumour's fortunate location, the impact of its removal was comparatively minimal. Erica was soon transferred from the Intensive Care Unit to a private ward. Erica noticed how right Gunnar had been. Eastern Europe seemed to have an impressive health care system, a far cry from the primitive expectations her arrogant western mind had entertained. She was sure that there were slightly less professionally run hospitals; Dr Adameck had explained how few experts on pancreatic surgery there were, so clearly this hospital was one of the more prestigious ones. Still, she was impressed.

After a week, she was considered fit enough to return to Prague to see Dr Adameck before she went home to her flat and life in Munich.

The company had asked her to provide a doctor's certificate to explain her sick leave but apart from that her mailbox was pretty empty. Dr Adameck had signed her off with depression and had prescribed her the newest pill as a cover, should any questions be asked. Neither Julia nor Gunnar had left any messages for her, which was both good and bad news. She missed Gunnar in some ways but his uncaring attitude had extinguished some of her feelings. Over the last few months she had become very dependent on him and she knew she would find it very hard to re-establish her life without him in it. She would give him a few more days to calm down before thinking about contacting him of her own accord. It would need to be done before she went back to work. Running into him without having cleared the air would be awkward and might draw unnecessary attention.

A few more days of recuperation at home were in order anyway.

Chapter 14

When Erica was sitting back in her home in Munich she decided to contact Arpan. After all, the cancer had come back and that meant that he owed her 87.97 % of her money, a sum that would help her nicely to recover from the huge dent the medical bills occurred in Prague and Kiev had made into her savings. Munich was not cheap to live in either, especially when much of the socialising was done with people who earned high salaries. She had been lucky that the company paid her so generously and so she had accrued a large amount of savings over the last two years.

Additionally, she would like to speak to Arpan about the cancer coming back and what he made of it. That was not supposed to happen and she could not wait to hear his explanation.

She was upset that Gunnar had not been in touch at all. The least he could do was to come up with a joint strategy as how to handle the split in public. How would he be when she saw him in the canteen? How about their mutual friends? Well, they were all really his. It was a mess that needed sorting out, and it didn't need much, simply a conversation between mature adults.

She could understand that he was overwhelmed by the idea of her healing – she would not have believed it herself had it not happened to her. However, that he should leave her just after she collapsed, without making sure that she was fine, she could not get over. All she wanted from him was the assurance that their private conflict would not cause awkwardness in the firm. If his behaviour was anything to go by, she expected him to give her the cold shoulder and to quietly withdraw from the social occasions that included her. That would suit her fine.

The operation had taken its toll on her. Erica was surprised about that, since her body was much fitter and her health much improved. She had been lucky to have found the tumour so early, before it had grown into an inoperable size. Still, she was shattered and it showed. When she asked her manager for some extra leave it was immediately granted.

"You look terrible," the woman in HR had said. "We need you back in shape, take as long as you need. I see from your note that you're on antidepressants. Maybe you want to speak to our research department if they have something better for you. I'm going to put you down for more sick leave. I have the certificate from the doctor in Prague and I can sign you off for a little longer. Maybe you should go somewhere sunny and warm, chill out by a beach or something. I hear sunshine helps as much as taking the tablets. Call us when you feel better."

"Thank you, I will."

She went to the research department to make her cover story convincing and signed up for a clinical study in two weeks' time. Until then she'd have all the time in the world to find Arpan.

It was a miracle that Julia hadn't magically appeared since Prague and seemingly knew nothing about either the cancer reoccurring or the operation. Overwhelmed by the diagnosis, Erica had acted in panic and she had feared what Julia might do. Erica had not been rational enough to make a sensible decision and had opted for the only safe option: getting the cancer out without any possible complications. It had cost her dearly but at least she had got it done.

Now that the whole affair was successfully finished and everything had been kept out of all of her official medical records, it seemed wise not to mention it. The only worry was Gunnar. Had he told anyone about it? He was unlikely to go into detail about the trip to Prague. Known as a very private person, he would either make no comment or explain their split in very general terms. She had tried to reach him a several times but he hadn't taken her calls and had not replied to any of her messages. She now had probably scared him even more into thinking that she was a crazy woman right out of 'Fatal Attraction'. Since Prague, his view of her had been shattered, there was no way to recover from that now.

Erica weighed her options. It was hard to imagine what Julia would do with all of this information. Would she attack Arpan publicly to discredit him completely? Would she fire Erica as soon as she could or would she keep it all in-house and use Erica as a laboratory rat? The secrecy would not go down well with the woman. The 'trust' between them had definitely been broken.

With that in mind Erica decided to make her way quietly to Wales without getting anyone else involved. She went to Paris on a train via Stuttgart, buying her ticket in cash so it would not show on her credit card details; she had long suspected that Julia had someone looking at her records. It would not be long before her credit card details would show the transactions in Kiev. Erica had to avoid that; once Julia smelled a rat, she would then be able to follow her paper trail.

She took the Eurostar to London St Pancras – what an evil coincidence having to pass a station with that name - splashed out on a cab for the short journey to Paddington and then took another train to Wales. Determined not to leave either a digital footprint or a witness, she left the train two stops early and took a bus and then a taxi from a village still quite far from Arpan's retreat. Should someone check the obvious local taxi companies for any fares between the train station and Arpan they wouldn't find anything. Exhausted from her travel she forced her way up the hill slowly until at long last she reached the gate.

The fence had been reinforced with barb wire and the gate was locked. There was no bell to ring so she was left to shouting for attention. She heard the familiar barking by Ashank and after a long wait she heard Anuj's voice:

"Who is it?"

"Erica Whittaker," she said, a tremble in her voice. "I need to speak to Arpan."

Anuj opened the gate slightly to have a look at her. "Are you alone?" he asked.

"Yes, I am," she said.

He opened the gate only a little, waved her to come inside quickly, and then locked the gate immediately.

"Your security measures have changed a little," she observed. "How come?"

"Just trying to keep to ourselves these days," Anuj explained as they walked towards the clearing. She noticed that everything apart from the fencing was unaltered.

"Where is Arpan?" she asked.

"Around here, somewhere. I'm not sure."

The two of them sat down on the tree trumps. Ashank immediately began to lick Erica's face enthusiastically.

"I'm glad to see that you did at least something to the gate," Erica said. "What's the point in having one if it is always open for anyone to just walk in?"

"We had no choice really," Anuj explained. "All of a sudden we had journalists show up at our doorstep. Turns out that someone wrote a book about Arpan and his healing experience with him. For one reason or another, some TV producer decided it was worth their while and they wanted to interview Arpan for a documentary programme. Needless to say we wouldn't have bothered but once some journalists had found us here and laid siege to the gate we had to put up the security system. In the end Arpan agreed to a short TV interview in exchange for the promise that they would leave us alone."

"Did it work?" she asked.

"In the long run it did. Things have died down now but at first it went ballistic. Arpan had not read the book and had no idea that he had been described as deluded and egotistical maniac who got lucky by a hysteric mass placebo effect. Since he hadn't practiced for 20 years that claim seemed to fit. By the way he'd been approached, Arpan had expected that he would be hailed as the saviour of the author's life – as he probably should be. The journalist tricked him into thinking it was a show about natural healing power. None of the preliminary discussions about the interview ever mentioned the angle they took, so he ran into a proverbial open knife."

"What happened?"

"Not that much. He was taken off guard and after 20 years of solitude he was no match for the blood-thirsty presenter. Arpan looked like the bad guy. It should have ended there but suddenly some of his other clients came out of the woodwork talking about his odd behaviour and the healing sessions that went along with the elixir injections. Instead of leaving it there and waiting for everything to die down again, he fell for this beautiful, charming woman who promised to have him on her show to set the record straight. When he went on TV she pulled up records of how much some people paid to be healed and of how some people died, despite of his treatment."

"How did that go down?" Erica asked.

"Not quite as badly as you would have thought. Arpan had prepared for such an event and could prove that most of his

146

money went to charities or to an account from where money was held so it could be used to reimburse his clients. Of course that was not the explosive TV that the producers had counted on and people probably switched off. After the first show the viewers had come to expect something more exciting, they wanted another public hate figure which they didn't quite get. The ratings and reactions were poor."

"So the storm is over?"

"Kind of. There've been a few unwanted visitors here since the information about his location leaked out there but it hasn't sparked off a strong interest. Of course, Arpan has taken it to heart. My mother says he used to be so strong and totally immune to criticism, now he's like an attention starved little child. The government has set up a committee to look into alternative healing some more but they can take years to come to a conclusion and proposals for new legislation."

"I'm actually with the public on the money issue," she said. "I can understand why the public are suspicious. I appreciate you have to be committed for the healing to work but it is a lot of money. He explained his reasons to me but I can see why it puts people off."

"Okay. Here's a hypothetical situation for you. Let's say you were like Arpan and could manually save about four people a day from certain, agonising death. Who would you choose?"

"What do you mean," she asked, taken aback. "I'd heal anyone I can, whoever comes into the door first."

"That's very sweet of you but don't you think that's unfair to the ones who came later, who were too busy looking after their children or elderly parents to make it to the front of the queue?" Anuj said provocatively. "The first ones will be the ones with helicopters and staff to help them find Arpan. That's hardly a fair criteria and a tough stance to take when you see the people who you have to turn down."

"Well, I guess I could give priority to the ones in biggest need, the ones with people who depend on them," Erica said.

"That means that all childless people are out, doesn't it?" he said.

She was beginning to feel uncomfortable with this conversation. "I guess, yes, that's what I'm saying."

"So we should have watched you die in agony for your lifestyle choices or because you were barren or had not found the right guy in time. Interesting point! What about children? They have no dependants."

"Of course you would save children because they have plenty of years of life ahead of them. You need to give children some kind of priority, too" Erica said, and now I can see where you are going with this."

"Good. So what about a 65 year old woman who looks after her grandchildren? How many years does she have to live, you reckon? Is she worth saving or not? And what about the millionaire who can leave his children a legacy, so they are taken care of. We can let him die, can't we?"

"I see your point," Erica said, "but to me that doesn't explain the exorbitant fees."

"Arpan couldn't solve the problem of how to choose the lucky ones. He meditated for an answer and couldn't find any guidance what so ever. He was very concerned about it and most upset to have that kind of power. In the end he used the money issue to deter as many people as possible. It was not ideal but at least he could be sure that these people were committed enough. He made some exceptions secretly."

"Anuj, when you're being diagnosed with cancer, terminal and nasty ones like pancreatic cancer especially, I think most of us will pay anything to stay alive. Anyone who knows the reality of cancer will be committed to the treatment. Regardless of his intentions, it looks as if Arpan wanted the money, and he was just being kind to the poor by not having a fixed fee but an income appropriate one."

"Well, it was seen by the TV viewers as money making and a rip off," Anuj continued.

"What about the success stories, the certificates and scan results? His successes speak for themselves? Did they not talk about that?"

"The successes are all 20 years in the past. It's easy to discredit something that happened so long ago. Many of the witnesses and his clients are dead by now anyway and it's easy to claim that it was all mass hysteria."

"There must have been people speaking up for him," Erica said.

"Of course they did, but the producers had an agenda and so they picked the most uneducated and vulnerable ones of Arpan's clients. None of the judges and lawyers or even doctors he had treated were invited, only simple minded, uneducated and unlikeable people; they did more harm than good."

"How is Arpan taking it?" Erica asked.

"Very badly. He's tried to remain calm but his energy has become completely unbalanced and unhinged. He's a mess."

Anuj left her and went looking for Arpan.

Erica stayed behind with the dog which was still making a huge fuss over her. She felt odd to be back at this ominous place. She had come here with a view to complain and to get her money back. The two years she had spent with scientists and the other staff at the company had done weird things to her mind. It still defied all belief. Gunnar's reaction, the TV shows – Erica could no longer make up her own mind how she felt about Arpan the whole healing thing, swayed by public opinion and confusion.

What had Arpan done to her and why had her cancer come back?

Part of her could not help but dismiss his ability and the elixir as total humbug and agree with the accusations of a mass hysteria and a hypnotic placebo effect, but another part of her could not deny the strong feelings she had had at the time and the scan results in London that had cleared her of all illness.

She used to laugh about people with strong faith in unbelievable phenomena. She remembered a long time ago when she went on a day trip to South London to meet a friend in a park. She found that the world and his brother were on the trains to the same location. Apparently a famous Indian woman who healed people by hugging them was giving an audience there. Thousands of people were on their way for just a few seconds with said lady, who did not even speak English. Erica had felt perturbed by the idea that grown up people in the 21st century would waste an entire day, travelling and queuing for a hug. She had found the whole thing so ridiculous, she contemplated giving out free hugs next to the entrance. Erica had been amazed when she saw that *regular* people going for this. The terms hippies and weirdoes again came to mind.

So was she one of these tree hugging people now or just cynical? She couldn't figure it out. One moment she was grateful for his help and good intentions, the next she got angry at him and suspicious.

"Amesh would like to see you," Anuj said suddenly. "Come with me."

He led Erica past the dome and into the woods, where Amesh was sitting on a blanket in a meditative position. The second she saw him in this peaceful pose she softened all up. With someone else, this pose might be seen as pretentious and showy but from him, she bought it. This man had something. What, she had no idea, but he had something. He was trying to connect with his inner self and become one with it. It was as if she could actually see the goodness in him. It was a shame he had returned to his 'Coward Boy' name. Was that really necessary?

"It's good to see you, Erica. I'm surprised to see you though," he said.

"I have a few questions for you," she said vaguely.

"I'm looking forward to answering them for you," he replied, not moving from his pose. "How have you been? Is Julia treating you alright? I am guessing that she doesn't know you're here."

"So you know about me and my work for the company? You're well informed, I grant you that," she said.

"Remember, Abby is still checking up on that orphanage for me. She tells me things off the record, which is a huge help when dealing with someone as manipulative and cold as Julia."

"You of all people must be able to see through her vulnerability and her inner hurt," Erica said provocatively.

"As a matter of fact, I do," Amesh said. "She should find a healer to help her with it, or at the very least, a good psychologist. Unfortunately, all I have to offer is pancreas related, and she might never need those services."

"Wouldn't it be great though if she got it and had to come here and beg you to help her?" Anuj said with a grin.

"I would not call it great," Amesh said, "but in my darker moments the thought has crossed my mind, too. It would be a good learning experience for her, but I wouldn't wish it on anyone."

"I have not seen much of Julia fortunately," Erica told him. "I work in Munich now at one of their plants, but the job is mainly clerical and I usually spend my time with more palatable people than her."

"Yet there must be a reason you came here. What can I do for you?" Amesh said, smiling gently but looking very tired. On closer examination she could see his hurt and fear. He had caught that air of vulnerability again which she had seen the first time she had come here.

"The cancer came back," Erica said.

Amesh leapt up from his lotus position and looked at her searchingly. His eyes scanned her body and her face for something, she was not sure what. He put his hand on her forehead and closed his eyes as if to read her mind.

Anuj looked shocked and disheartened at the two of them.

"Well, you rushed her treatment and you never got to finish it off," he tried to defend his master.

"That's not strictly true," Amesh said. "I did everything I could possibly do. This should not have happened."

"Well it bloody well has and I want my money back," she said, feeling a lot of anger welling up inside her. Her initial warm feelings and sympathy for the man had disappeared and been replaced by rage against someone who looked so incompetent all of a sudden. "My entire life has changed because of this."

"Your life changed because of the cancer, not because of us. If you had taken the warning from your body seriously and changed your life then maybe you would not have grown the tumour back," Anuj said coldheartedly.

"Enough Anuj," his master told him. "You can have your money back, of course," he replied to Erica. "I always promised you that and I will stick to my word."

"And I will take you up on that now," she said. "Have you got no explanation to offer why this happened to me?" she asked. "Is it possible the treatment did not work because of who I am?"

"I don't think so," Amesh said and shook his head slowly. "I really think that I am more evolved than this. Healing always comes first in my life and I don't hate you for what has happened."

"Couldn't it affect you subconsciously?" she asked. "Clearly something has gone wrong."

"It must have, but I don't understand why."

"That was an odd joke that you left me 12.03% of my money anyway. Why was that?"

"Oh yes," Amesh said slowly. "It wasn't a joke. It was a gesture of reconciliation. 12th March. I thought you'd get that."

"Of course," she replied. "How stupid of me not to get that reference. You used the date of the accident. So you knew all along – before Julia told you? Maybe your feelings weren't so pure after all or, not charging your full fee has altered your powers?"

"Anything is possible, as we both have learned," Amesh said cryptically. "I shouldn't think that matters, though, because my energy was pure and fully committed. I healed a few clients in the past without charging any money. None of them had ever complained. You're the only one who was healed and then had the cancer return," he assured her. "Anuj, get the elixir ready. The only thing I can offer Erica is to repeat my treatment. I will still reimburse the 87.97% in any case."

"Thank you for the money," Erica said. "I will happily take it. I should probably tell you though that I have had surgery and had the cancer removed but the cash will come in handy with my medical bills."

"I'd still like to treat you," Amesh said suddenly.

Erica looked at him with astonishment. How could he do that as Amesh, she wondered. Her first instinct was to decline his offer. Why fix something when it wasn't broken? She was in the clear. His first treatment had worked on her, at least for two years, so she couldn't dismiss all of his ability, but at the same time the cancer had come back. Could the elixir do her harm now? She remembered the pain, the cramps and the nausea and she didn't feel ready for it. Especially since her body still felt so bad and she had scar tissue that probably needed more time still to heal.

"How long would this last?" she asked. "Is it another ten day course?"

"Like last time, it would be a ten day course in the space of five," he said. "You would have to stay here for the duration. I'm not letting you go outside again and be seen by that nosy B&B woman."

"Maybe the quickening of the treatment rendered it short term?" Erica pointed out. "Do you really think it is a good idea?"

"We can do it in ten if you like," Amesh offered. "Does anyone know that you're here?"

"Not this time," she replied. "I'm on sick leave, but nobody knows that the cancer reoccurred, not even that I ever had it. The diagnosis and the surgery were done in Eastern Europe, so well out of Julia's reign. Only a childish ex-boyfriend has heard of it but he thinks I'm lying or have lost my mind. He'll be too embarrassed to talk about it with anyone. "

"What about Julia? Are you sure she knows nothing?"

"She knows nothing yet and it would be an odd coincidence if she suddenly decided to check up on me now. However, there is a remote possibility that she might find out if she were to check my financial transactions. The surgery in Kiev would be a giveaway."

"How come she has access to your financial records?" Anuj asked surprised.

"If she sets her mind to it, a woman like Julia is able to obtain that kind of information; it's just a question of whether she would ever do that or not," Amesh replied. "Stranger things have happened, but let's hope that her mind is otherwise engaged. So are you in or out?" he asked Erica.

"I have nothing to lose, of course I'm in. Just be careful with the scar."

Chapter 15

Erica wondered about the whole healing philosophy. If Arpan had been right that there was this spiritual element to his treatments, then why was she the first person to have the cancer reoccur? What had he done wrong in his sessions with her? The doubt and fear gnawed away at her and she was reluctant to offer her arm for the next injection of the elixir.

"What's wrong?" Anuj asked. "Why are you flinching?"

"I don't know."

"Relax, and let me and Arpan take care of you," he tried to soothe her.

"Back to Arpan again," she said with a hint of cynicism.

"You have that effect on him," Anuj said, with that now familiar wink.

"How can I be sure that you don't mean me harm?" she asked.

"Why would you even think that?" Anuj asked taken aback.

"Because of who I am," Erica said. "Because of our history."

"Do you think that a person as evolved as Arpan would let some old grievance interfere with his one mission in life, to heal others?" Anuj asked. "Get a grip on reality. Maybe I would find it difficult to forgive you but not Arpan."

"Thank you, Anuj," Arpan said. "I think we need to get this entire thing out into the open now before we proceed. Erica, I never blamed you for what you did. You were very young, you had just lost your parents in a most tragic way – you needed to take it out on someone. I always understood that and I never blamed you. This kind of thing doesn't affect how I feel about any of my clients or how committed I am to the healing."

"I'm glad you see it that way. I've often regretted my actions ever since," Erica admitted sheepishly. "I was out of order. At first I was motivated by revenge. Everyone in the accident had died, so I had nobody to blame. You became the obvious target for my anger and grief. I didn't think once about how you must have felt. It wasn't fair to add to your misery in the way I did. You were suffering from bereavement, too. By the time I understood the entire situation more fully, I had of course spent all the money you paid in the settlement. I'd been on a trip around the world, got myself a fancy car had built up huge bar tabs all over London, otherwise I would have considered reimbursing you: I felt always guilty about that."

"You now know well that I could easily afford paying," Arpan said reassuringly. "Money was no object and I was happy to part with it so the entire affair would not be dragged out and nobody would connect Arpan with the accident. Your anger corresponded with my own feelings in many ways."

"Really?" she asked surprised.

"I felt responsible for the accident," he explained, looking at the floor. "My son and his mother were irresponsible in their actions and that led to the death of four people. How could I not feel bad about what my family had done to yours? Additionally, I was so wrapped up in my own grief that I couldn't have cared less about money."

"I'm still sorry for letting my aggressive lawyer loose on you," she said.

"Unlike yours, my way of dealing with the situation was to bury my head in the sand and pretend that nothing had happened: I settled out of court to protect my privacy. I tried to accept my loss by endless hours filled by meditation and isolating myself from everyone around me. Me shutting everyone out broke up my relationship and landed me with a lifelong enemy and that enemy is not you."

Anuj looked confused.

"Relationship?" he wondered out loud. "I didn't know you were ever in a relationship?"

"I was briefly. At the time when my son and his mother died in that car accident, I had a girlfriend but she became so frustrated and jealous of my grief that she broke up with me."

"I'm so sorry," Erica said and began to cry. "All I thought about was that she should not have let her son drive the car without a licence and that it was the fault of your wife and son that my parents died in a crash that should never have happened. Everyone told me to seek justice. I never thought about you and your loss and what it would do to your life."

"I don't blame you to this day for your hurt. You were young, that kind of reaction was to be expected from you. You always had and always will have my sympathy for it," he said.

"The accident was unnecessary, it hurts me for your parents just as much as for my own family. It was my son's fault for driving, his mother's for letting him drive and mine for being so absent in their lives that they lost their way and acted so foolishly. I never took what you did personally, you never met me face to face, only my lawyers. You were within your rights to seek justice and compensation and I was happy to oblige."

"What happened to the girlfriend?" Erica asked.

"Things weren't going well between us anyway," Arpan said casually. "I was busier than ever with the clinic and she always complained and nagged me to spend more time with her. I was in my forties, she was much younger and wanted to have a child with me as soon as possible, so that our child wouldn't have too old a father. She hated that I spent so much time with the healing. I almost wanted to break it off because I felt my calling was more important than a relationship anyway. How could I have a cosy night at home with the TV and turn down dying people begging for my help? How could she not see that I had no choice! How could I not use every possible minute of my day to help people? How could I stop when that meant the certain death for a person? She could never understand that, so how good a match would we have been in the long run? I was thinking of setting her free, so she could find a man who could give her what she needed. That man was not me."

"You make it sound like like you are a slave to your gift," Erica said.

"In a way I am," he said. "How can you ever justify not using it?"

"You did stop using it," Erica pointed out.

"You are right, I did," Arpan admitted. "That's quite a different story but first I need to explain to you why there are no hard feelings. Well, the girlfriend and I were arguing a lot and when the accident killed all of our loved ones, I felt empty inside. It was a miracle that the press never connected me and my child. Thomas's birth certificate used my civilian name and as you know, nobody ever put two and two together. The car was also registered in that name. That part of the story never broke, it was Whittaker against Wilson; Wilson always represented by his lawyers. No court case and no face to be photographed and to be recognised. Instead I hid more than ever in my healing, working

156

ever more punishing hours. My girlfriend left me and had a child with someone else. It was all for the better. She hates me but she got what she wanted most in life: a child. After just losing one I would never have agreed to have another."

"Do you not feel guilty about it?" Erica asked. "You seem to have broken her heart."

"I feel bad and sorry for her, but mainly because she had developed this unhealthy attachment to me and our union. She would have been happier if she could just get on with her life, if she had fallen in love with the father of her children and if she had allowed herself to get past this and enjoy her life. She chose self-imprisonment and voluntary bitterness. She put me on a pedestal and cultivated the loss for the rest of her life. Whenever I see her, she's full of hate. I wish I could heal that hurt but she won't let me. It's a waste of a life. For that I'm sorry and for failing her, but to sacrifice a human life or several so that I could massage her needy ego and to give her all the cuddles that she needed, while next door someone is dying, what choice did I have?"

"You're not responsible for all pancreatic cancer," Erica said.

"I know, but it seemed important to do as much as I could."

"So why did you stop?" Erica asked. "This orphanage story seems less and less convincing."

"I began to fail. When I first started I had a near 100% success rate and only a handful of failures during almost my entire healing career; suddenly I was failing at least one patient a week."

"Don't say fail," Anuj interjected.

"No, Anuj. I failed. I was not concentrating hard enough, not meditating enough, not eating or sleeping enough. An emptiness ate me from the inside and I refused to deal with it. For a highly evolved and aware human being, I was a mess and a complete let down."

"You can't beat yourself up over it. You are human and can only do so much," Anuj replied.

"I won't hide behind excuses. The drug companies pressured the government and the people who had been protecting me let me know that the increasing rate of failure tied their hands. There was no licence for the kind of thing I do and my enemies were building a case around the failures and the fees I charged. When Julia's predecessor came and offered me the deal it was a feeble excuse to justify giving up. I was exhausted really. The week prior to the day that I signed the contract, I received four claims to return the money. Four people died because of my fading powers. It was devastating to see the smashed hopes in their faces, to see the anger and bitterness of those whose lives would end in the most horrible way. Seeing their fear and knowing I could not help them, it was complete torture."

"You must have hated me for pushing you so hard at the time," Erica said. "I'm so sorry."

"I didn't even notice you pushing me. Your legal threat was the least of my worries. I felt terrible for you and you are welcome to all the money that I paid you. If it helped only a little to lessen your pain, then I'm very pleased with it."

"If I had known who you were…" she began.

"Then you would have taken a bigger cut," Anuj ended the sentence for her and Erica looked guiltily to the floor.

"Water under the bridge," Arpan said warmly.

"There's only one person who hates Arpan," Anuj said," and that's my mother. I guess I know now who that girlfriend was and why my mother argues with you all the time."

Arpan went and hugged Anuj. "For what it's worth, she had a better life with your father than with me. I could never have given you the same stable upbringing as he did. I'm here for you now."

"So the deal with the drug company was only a façade?" Erica asked.

"I traded lives, in big numbers. My personal actions could only heal a few people each week, however hard I worked. When this emptiness took hold of me and my confidence dwindled I became susceptible to the persuasions of the drug company. Avoiding a public shaming, a counting out of the deaths I felt were on my hands, legal hearings about malpractice and licences… I knew in my heart of hearts that I could not win this battle. Now I was presented with a possibility of a deal from a huge pharmaceutical company, saving hundreds as many lives each week. I had turned them down many times, thinking that with all the money I was making from my patients that I would be able to save many lives myself. I donated money to charity and to cancer research. Those were large sums, definitely enough to make a difference, but when the company offered to dole out HIV medication to patients in Africa who otherwise would never have the chance of getting them at affordable prices, I had to accept; they promised generous policy changes in Africa on top of that. It played up to my ego to think I could make such a difference in the world. You know how much the companies charge for good combination drug therapy and how nobody in developing countries can afford that kind of treatment: the lucky ones get used as guinea pigs in trials. My signature changed the lives of so many for the better. In a weak moment of delusion or maybe desperation I signed, honestly thinking that this trade had tipped the balance of life enough to justify my retirement. A retirement I thought would be forced upon me soon anyway but I came to regret it. It dawned on me much later that those human drug experiments that the company promised me to stop would now be happening somewhere else, maybe in Asia, but they would still do them somewhere. Who is to say whether I succeeded and made the right choice? I'm still not sure about it."

"So what do you think you should have done?" Erica asked.

"I just don't know," Arpan said quietly, full of emotion. "I wish I knew what I should have done. I was no longer sure of my healing powers. That former certainty of mine being taken away was a simple mathematical equation of lives and deaths. I thought I had no choice but did I? Could I have driven a harder bargain, saved more lives, more children? I now had blood on my hands, that of pancreatic cancer patients that otherwise would have been saved, albeit only a few of them. Every day over the last 20 years that I was sitting in meditation, doing nothing but my own little unimportant daily routines, I was letting people die instead of helping them."

"That's the drug company's fault," Anuj said agitatedly. "They are the ones who blackmailed you."

"They are in the same dilemma," Arpan said. "There are many good souls in those companies and many remarkable people. They, too, have their limits. Maybe there are frequent nasty underhand dealings going on but the companies can also only do so much. They could always save more people and spend more money on charitable projects, but they are corporations with employees, shareholders and bills to be paid. They face competition, they need money for research and experiments. They, too, have to make life and death decisions on a daily basis. It's a heavy burden to carry and we mustn't assume that those making the decisions don't feel the weight, the guilt and the pain."

"Arpan, it's great that you see the goodness in everyone and everything, but you're talking about huge corporations here, who rarely are benign entities," Erica said. "I'm working for them now and I have a pretty good idea what they're up to. It leaves a lot to be desired for."

"They've been good to you, have they not," Arpan argued. "They could have handled you and me quite differently. You see, there is goodness to some degree. There is always more that can be done, agreed. Tell me: where do you want them to draw the line? Stop paying the shareholders until they take their money elsewhere? Paying a pittance to scientists until they go elsewhere? Make you work like slaves for minimum wages and spend every possible penny in saving lives?"

"Why not?" Anuj said emotionally. "Shouldn't we all?"

"If nobody dies, we won't have enough space and resources on the planet," Erica said.

"Exactly," Arpan said. "Only you don't want to die, the kids in Africa don't want to die and neither do I. So who is to decide who gets to live?"

"You had 20 years to think about that," Erica said. "You must have come to a conclusion about it."

"As a matter of fact, I have," Arpan said. "When the contract is fulfilled I will start practising again but I will also try and train other people how to heal. I will pour all of my resources into passing on that gift. I regret having entered into an arena of politics and policy decisions that are against everything I stand for. I was given this gift and that is all I will be thinking about in the future. I will leave it to others to make deals and contracts with lives. It has upset me too much, the price is too high for a sensitive soul like myself and nobody is to say that any of the trading leads to anything. Companies are just not transparent enough to make them a good business partner."

160

"It seems to me as though you're still grieving Thomas and Erin," Erica said. "You clearly have never dealt with it properly. You're a good healer, but are you receiving healing yourself?"

"I had 20 years to think about it and sort out my head," Arpan said dismissively. "If you ask Anuj's mother, I took more time than necessary for it."

"It still leaves me wondering why my cancer came back," Erica said. "In all the newspaper cuttings that I read about you, you never once had a reoccurrence. Failure, yes, but reoccurrence, no; it was either all or nothing with you."

"I wish I knew why that is. It has nothing to do with you and me as far as my feelings are concerned. I don't bear grudges with individuals for their own personal shortcomings. We are all human beings. Corporations and society are driven by those individuals, so we are bound to make mistakes and wrong decisions."

"You're too good to be true," Erica said. "It's wonderful that you're so positive and forgiving, but can any human being be that good? Your subconscious at least must be human like the rest of us. Few can find that amount of inner strength to forgive."

"I won't argue with that, but I believe that my excessive meditating has helped me reach a serene point in my life where I could let go of it all."

"You were under a lot of pressure to finish my treatment before Julia found us. You might not have finished it as well as you would have under less tense circumstances," Erica pointed out.

"That's not how it felt," he said sternly. "It lasted two years for you. All I can do now is to try again and repeat the treatment."

Erica was visibly weighing her options before committing to it with a weak but steady nod of her head.

"All I ask you is to open your mind to the possibility that what I'm doing is correct."

"I believe you," she said after a short break. She was tired from all the talking and arguing and all she wanted was to sleep. "Go ahead," she added with a devil may care attitude.

The needle pierced her skin and found its way into a vein. The burning was worse than she ever had felt. A wild tingling sensation spread from the inside of her elbow towards the rest of her arm. It felt more like blood was draining from her arm and the arm became lifeless and numb. Within seconds her shoulder and neck were affected and then her other arm and then the rest of her torso; all she could feel now was her head, disproportionally big. She had no idea where her body had gone, she couldn't even see it. At last the tingling sensation arrived at the back of her head and she gradually lost her consciousness; she emerged into nothingness and appreciated it. No thoughts and no sensations other than a general pleasantness and relaxation. It was fantastic, exactly what she had longed for.

When she came back to her senses she ached badly. It was again this terrible hangover feeling with a splitting headache and an unpleasant clogginess in every pore of her skin, combined with nausea and clamminess.

"You had a lot of toxins in your body," Arpan told her when he saw that she was awake. "That nasty anaesthetic was still lingering and lots of harmful substances from God knows what medication and food you've been feeding yourself lately. All I could do was flush that out of your system. The real work will not start until tomorrow."

"We don't have a lot of time," Erica said agitatedly, concerned about the dragging out of this violent treatment. "At some point Julia will notice that I'm gone and she is bound to look here first."

"That's possible but if she finds out that you've had surgery in Kiev it is unlikely that she will suspect you're here. We rushed the last treatment and, as you rightfully pointed out, this could have had something to do with the cancer coming back. I don't think it is likely but we should not take any more chances. We are going to do this properly this time."

Erica suddenly had the urge to throw up and ran towards the edge of the clearing to do the inevitable out of everyone's view but she never made it. The spasms of her stomach were violent and uncontrollable and she feared that her scar might split. Exhausted she let herself sink onto the grass when she was done.

"God, sometimes the hurt of being cured by you feels just as bad as the original pain from the cancer," she said. "I feel like dying right now."

162

Arpan smiled at her.

"I know it's bad. I'm sorry I can't spare you the pain, only the death part at the end of it, if things work out. Have some water and rest. I have animals to attend to," he said and left her to it.

She stayed on the floor for a little longer but then she began to feel the moisture seeping through her clothes and she got up to get changed in the dome. She had only brought a backpack and had little in the way of a wardrobe. If she were here for ten days, she would have to find a way to wash things. She wondered how Arpan and Anuj did their laundry. They had only a small generator for energy which would not be enough for a washing machine, not that she had ever seen one, but in all the time she had spent here, she had not seen a washing line or anything that implied they were doing it manually either. Well, something else to find out.

Her scar was throbbing even though on closer inspection it seemed perfectly fine. Once she was dressed in clean clothes she lay down on the mattress and fell asleep.

Chapter 16

When she awoke it was dark. She heard Arpan chanting outside the dome, only him, not Anuj as well. Erica took a mental inventory of her body and her pain. It wasn't too bad now, the nausea had been the worst part and that had subsided. She would have to eat something soon but she hated to interrupt Arpan in his practice. She had brought nothing to eat. She wondered what the two men usually ate and what they would offer her.

At long last Arpan was done with the singing, came into the dome and switched on the lights.

"I'm sorry about the noise but I had a feeling that I had better bring you around and feed you before you woke up in the middle of the night and wouldn't be able to find anything."

He handed her a bowl with salad and a single banana. She greedily gulped it down.

"Where is Anuj?" she asked. "It must have come as quite a shock that you and his mother used to go out with each other. Is he alright?"

"He's gone off to meditate and process the information, I guess. It was quite a shock, that was obvious, but I think once he has had time to digest the news it will have a positive effect on him. He always wondered why she and I never got on well. At least now he has a better understanding of the complexity of the situation. We should have told him ages ago but his mother is very difficult to reason with and she insisted I should play no role in his life; that was until she changed her mind and literally dumped him here. She can't cope with the fact that he and I get on. He approves of what I do and has chosen to become my disciple and apprentice. I appreciate her frustration, seeing the man you wanted to have a family with being close to the son he should have fathered with you. We are the family she wanted, but she is not part of it. Anuj forfeits his own life for the purpose of learning how to heal. Other kids like him spend their time dating and chasing girls, but he's chosen to live an ascetic life. I'm confident he won't be bearing any grudges over it. If anything, he might feel compassion for his mother. When he came to me, he really hated her."

"He must still be grieving for his little brother. How did that accident happen?"

"His mother was speaking on her mobile phone and didn't look where her little one was walking. He ran onto the road and got hit by a car. That's why he hates her so much, he holds her responsible. Also, she drove her second husband out of the house with her bitterness and anger. Anuj grew up in a toxic environment but he's a survivor. Fortunately here, Anuj has learned to channel his energy in a much more constructive way and has learned to heal himself. I have high hopes for him; he started young and is very gifted."

"Is that what you're trying to do with him, build a legacy?"

"I would like that, yes. Not so much a personal cult but a passing on of what I have learned. I spent vast amounts of time with healers from all over the world to learn from them. What I have experienced and what they taught me has become my technique, a mixture of various methods and ideas. I had this family history with pancreas disease, that organ would not let me go and I achieved a breakthrough there. I'm trying to figure out if Anuj can do the same. He, too, has a family connection with the pancreas. He has witnessed what I have done with you and subsequently I've managed to tell him all about it."

"Are you saying that I served as a guinea pig for him?" she asked with suspicion. Had Arpan really done the healing himself, or had he let Anuj do it for him and could that be the reason why the cancer had come back? Anuj had said that Arpan was forgiveness but he had never made the same statement about himself. She wondered if the young man hated her, which would have probably influenced his commitment to the healing, too.

"You were a case study, but no, he did no healing on you. He observed what I did, his time for hands on healing won't come until he has seen many more cases like yours. With all of my teachers, they never let me get involved until very late into my studies. He would not be ready yet, you don't have to worry about that."

Erica was a little relieved but not entirely at ease. Arpan switched off the light and settled down to sleep, leaving her with her thoughts in the dark.

Again she woke to chanting outside the dome. It was almost morning, although not even five a.m. She discerned two voices this time so Anuj had obviously come back from his introspection.

"I'm glad you are up," Arpan said to Erica as he came into the dome. "It's time for the elixir," he said and prepared the injection. Anuj had not joined them and immediately Erica had an odd feeling about this.

"Is Anuj avoiding me?" she asked.

"Of course not. He's feeding and looking after the animals," Arpan explained. "Stop being so paranoid. He and I had a long chat this morning. He'll be joining us shortly."

"I guess being at death's doorstep for a second time around makes you worry too much," she said half-jokingly.

"I know, we've come to your trust issues all over again," he said. "It's time for the blindfold," he said and tied a bandana over her eyes. He injected the elixir, which this time created only a mild discomfort and felt oddly cool in her veins, but she was struggling to be sure of any definite sensation associated with it at all. Maybe the elixir needed the tumour to make an impact?

Arpan pulled on her other hand, indicating that he wanted her to get up and follow him, but he didn't speak. He gently guided her outside the dome and into the woods, or at least that was what she thought he was doing. She soon lost her sense of orientation completely but she knew that this was what the session was all about, so she tried to let go of her unease and just go with it.

It was clearly a variation of the session they had done with her two years ago that had left her alone and abandoned in the woods. This time she was not only prepared for it, she would not be scared into any primal emotions, of that she was certain. Knowing what to expect was a great comfort and so she was happy to follow his lead, confident and almost cocky. All she needed was a little patience to sit this session out. They would leave her somewhere in the woods and wait for her to panic. Well, they could wait a long time for that, she thought to herself.

She stumbled and almost fell over some tree roots, another indication that she was right in her assumptions. A few scratches from bushes and branches got her to realise that Arpan was leading her somewhere along the edge of the clearing rather than into the woods. He finally got her to sit down against a tree trunk and then his hands were on her temples, radiating heat into her.

166

The force of it was unbelievable and almost threatening. It felt as if her head was going to burst. She wanted to grab his arms and pull the hands away but someone, Anuj presumably, was holding her arms down and tied them together behind her back. She had a vague sensation that the same was done to her feet, rendering her completely immobile. It sprang to her mind once again how odd all of these eccentric measures must have been for the first few patients who had come to seek help for their illness. Just how many of those initial clients had let him willingly do such things to them? She briefly remembered the story of a retired High Court judge. The picture of him in the paper showed such an imperial, arrogant and old public school man. How would he have dealt with this experience of helplessness and submission? But her thoughts started to get muddled and disjointed. The tension she felt in her head became a huge ringing noise that made it impossible to ignore. If she had learned one thing from all the treatments two years ago then it was to offer no resistance and to let everything just happen naturally to her.

"You destroyed my family," she heard Anuj suddenly say, although she could not discern for sure if that was inside her head or whether he was for real.

"I'm sorry," she tried to say but the words did not come out. "Anuj, please…"

"You are going to die here," she heard a man say. His voice familiar and she knew, she knew the voice, then it hit her: Mike, it was Mike her former boss from the agency in Canary Wharf talking. It was a relief to establish for a fact that she was imagining things. Anuj might be here, but Mike simply could not be.

"You're just a trick of my mind, you sexist idiot!" she said.

"You're wrong about that," Mike replied. "I'm here alright. I had to pay you that courtesy. I always fancied you, you know that, and you were a great worker. I've always been one for honesty and you need to be told that this mumbo-jumbo isn't going to do you any good!"

"Leave me alone," she shouted.

"Oh, you are angry with me for letting you go, aren't you? How sweet of you to care," he said playfully. "Well, I'm afraid that an account like that of Julia's is worth your death a few times over. You must know that. It doesn't mean I don't care. It's okay,

just let go and Arpan will help you to the other side. Surrender…
surrender.”

"You big fat liar," she screamed but she felt that he had
gone already. Not gone, of course, but drifted out of her mind
with his imaginary presence. It was just like him to be so tasteless.

"I tried my best," she now heard Hilda speak as clearly as if
her former assistant was standing right in front of her.

"Hilda, you angel. Whatever happened to you? I miss you!"
Erica called out.

"I'm so sorry, my dear. I was misled. I thought I had
brought you to a competent man, but it seems he doesn't know
the first thing he's doing, does he? I'm very, very sorry. This is all
my fault. I'll make sure they put that in your obituary."

"What is your fault? Without you I would never have met
the man. I would have died two years ago."

"Really? Is that what you think? Is it really two years
already? You know that isn't true. The man has no power
whatsoever. What you felt is all an illusion. You're dying, Erica.
You're dying now. That's why you can hear me and Mike. We
came to say our goodbyes."

As she was listening to Hilda, she began to feel as if she
truly was in a hospital bed. Was this hypnosis?

"Whatever happened to you, Hilda? I haven't seen you in
all that time…"

"I've been coming here almost every day," Hilda said,
sounding very hurt. "You're still that selfish and ungrateful bitch
of a woman that tried to get ahead in the company and never
cared about me. Go, rot in hell!"

"Come back!" Erica called out as she felt her assistant
disappear.

"She's not coming back," Julia's voice suddenly said loud
and clear. "Why would she come back?"

"I know I treated her badly, but she has forgiven me since,"
Erica said in tears.

"Keep telling yourself that," Julia said coldly. "That was
just an illusion. Hilda was so pleased when you left, she brought
in cake every day for an entire week."

"Leave me alone," Erica said angrily. "You don't know
Hilda."

"Oh I know Hilda well," Julia said with sadistic pleasure.

"Go away!" Erica screamed.

"I wish I could, but I'm here to shatter your illusions that you were healed, to bring you back to reality, which is that you have cancer, that you are helplessly stuck in a hospital bed with tubes coming out of your body, you're strapped to the bed so that you won't hurt yourself when your pain convulsions come again. Today is the day you are going to die and your dream of a miracle rescue and Arpan has come to an end. Who would even choose such a name? I admire your imagination, my dear. You should have become a playwright or something. For heaven's sake, woman, get a grip on reality. He isn't real."

"You're not real," Erica said, tears beginning to flood from her eyes. "You're not real, you can't be."

"If you think so, then it must be so," Julia said with an arrogant laugh that rocked Erica to her core.

"Stop it," Erica begged between tears. "Stop it."

"The truth is hard to bear," Julia said. "Be glad that I had the decency to tell you what is really going on. At least you'll die knowing. Goodbye now. I'll see you in hell!"

Erica wanted to rip off her blindfold to see what was real and what was not. She didn't know any more what to believe. Nothing seemed real.

"You have to untie her now," she heard Anuj say. "This is enough."

"No," she heard Arpan say next to him. "Leave her a little longer. She responded strongly and I hope there is more that will come up to the surface. I think there might be a little more for her to explore."

"I'm awake now," Erica said and promptly Anuj took her blindfold off.

She trembled from her emotions. "Thank God I'm here. What a nightmare. For a second I really thought I was in a hospital dying."

"Bad dreams are far more helpful than good ones will ever be," Anuj said. "You can learn a lot from your fears. It's perfectly normal for you to think about death so much that it infiltrates your dreams."

He untied her and took off the blindfold.

"Thank you," she said with a huge sigh of relief but she saw him in a different light now. What she imagined he had said in

169

her dreams stayed clearly with her and she could not help but feel a big chasm had opened between them now.

She gathered all of her courage and told the two men exactly what she had experienced. Anuj just grinned and put his hand on her shoulder. She looked at Arpan, hoping for a reassuring gesture but he sat there listening without giving away any of his thoughts or emotions.

"I'm surprised that with all the people who came through, my boyfriend Gunnar never made an appearance in my dream. I loved him for two years and he didn't have anything to say in my nightmare. I'm so angry at him for dumping me the way he did. Is that a good thing or bad that he had no role in this dream?"

"I guess that session today was not about anger or trust, as I had expected. It was about your fears: naturally they stop you from loving and trusting. You seem to have a lot of those fears by the sound of it. Gunnar probably never had the time to come through, even if he wanted to, but maybe he simply poses no threat to you. Try to get in touch with your feelings about these people and have a good think about what you fear from them."

"Hilda has just disappeared, but I miss her, not fear her. Mike, that seems such a long time ago, I'm surprised he should make an appearance at all. I never had anything to fear from him. Just Julia but that is no surprise."

"You should at least try. You might be surprised how sometimes people are prepared to share their truth with you, if you approach them correctly."

"So what about you, Anuj," she asked. "You were in my dream, too. You said you hated me for destroying your family."

"That is true, in principle," he said. "I could have been Arpan's son. I would have preferred that. My mother never got over him, which is why she is such a horrible person. But I have realised and accepted that Arpan would not have married my mother or fathered another child in any case. The accident and its legal aftermath only accelerated the process of them splitting up and probably are the reason I was conceived at all."

"So why was I dreaming about Hilda and Mike?"

"Feelings don't always go where your mind tells them to," Arpan said. "They can be irrational. You placed your life into Hilda's hands, Mike was steering your career. They all had power over you, more than you acknowledge. Gunnar probably didn't.

170

The main thing is that your fears have come to the surface, where you can deal with them. It goes to show that the treatment worked."

"I feel that, too," Erica added with a brave but unconvincing smile.

Arpan nodded thoughtfully.

"The best way to get you out of your head now and back into your feelings is to distract you with something more pleasant," he said. "You are on goat duty now, go and milk the goat. That can be good fun," he added.

She didn't have much luck with the goat and in the end Arpan let her off and gave her a ball to throw for the dog, who was a grateful game partner and never seemed to tire. His eager excitement helped Erica to forget about the last few hours and regain perspective on her life. It had been a rollercoaster of emotions. Nightmares could be very scary, even when one knew they were not real. She felt that she had come out stronger and didn't feel the need to meet anyone and discuss her fears and feelings. She would be alright.

In the evening, the three of them sat by the fire in silence. It was unusual and uncomfortable for her not to speak with people for such a long time but she was tired and needed the mental rest.

Chapter 17

The next week came and went quickly without much drama. Arpan treated her every other day but since the session with her nightmares there had been no more pain and nothing so dramatic. To her, the rest of the treatment felt like pleasant massages and meditations. Erica slept through most of them and felt sleepy and drowsy for most of the days, too. She got used to doing nothing between sessions and to the quiet life that the two men led here with little to no conversation between them.

If it were not for the basic nature of the living conditions, she could have mistaken her stay for a spa holiday. It was much more like she always had expected a healer to work: less intrusive physically and mentally. Since she didn't have a tumour, she was spared the unbelievable sensation of a psychic surgery. She had been afraid of having to go through that part of the treatment. Although most sessions had been painful, that was the one stuck out on her memory as the worst.

By her own calculations, she had two more days to go here before the course was complete and her treatment sealed. Her trust in Arpan had been resurrected as had her confidence of coming out of this fully cured.

It was during this happy moment that Anuj suddenly came running to the dome and announced: "We have visitors. There are people by the gate. The camera just sent me a warning."

"Who could it be?" Erica asked, but she had a feeling that she already knew.

"Might be just some journalists again, or one of the neighbours asking about a border fence or something mundane," Arpan said and got up to answer the call. "That kind of thing happens too you know. Not just drama and threats."

"I bet it is Julia," Erica said. "She came in halfway through my last treatment, too. That woman has a sixth sense when it comes to messing up my life," she added.

"If it is her then you still have nothing to worry about. We will hide you like we did before. This time she cannot be sure that you are here because you didn't leave a trail. Only the taxi driver would know about you, and you picked one from a different train station. You covered your tracks very well."

"I'd feel better though if I could be sure."

"Arpan will be back any moment now, and then we'll know. If you're that worried, go and hide behind the dome."

Erica did just that and waited there.

"You can come out," she heard Anuj call eventually, and when she came out from behind the dome he continued: "It was just that B&B woman, Mrs Jones. Apparently it's been noted that you're missing, so the lovely lady was just checking in to hear if you by chance had come here. No cause for alarm just yet."

"I wouldn't say that," Arpan admitted. "I don't know if she believed me. A busybody like her always smells a rat, even if there isn't one."

"Well, we'd better crack on with the treatment then," Erica said impatiently. "I don't want this course interrupted, too. If Julia has noticed that I'm missing, it won't be long until Gunnar tells her about our fall out and what I told him in Prague about the healing. That's not going to go down well with her; it will lead her to the clinic in Prague, to Kiev and eventually back here. It is obvious that I would come here."

"It is obvious to you, but not to her. It wasn't even obvious to us. God only knows what she will make of the news that your cancer had returned. If she hears of my failure it should please her but hopefully won't lead her to the conclusion that you came here of all places. If the first treatment I gave you failed, then why would you come here for more? It makes no sense, does it? You came here to confront me, not for more treatment. For you to trust me once again is something she would never grasp."

"No," Anuj interrupted. "It will make sense to her. She thinks like a predator and counts on fear and desperation. They are not unreasonable feelings to expect and they lead to all kind of irrational behaviour."

"Well, if she does come here, it will be on a hunch and it should be easy to deflect her. I still think that all she would be after is proof of my incompetence. The clinic in Prague would probably leak their documents to her for the right price. That will be the end of me and the 'myth' around me," Arpan said in a much more amused tone than Erica thought was appropriate.

"You are taking the news remarkably well," she observed.

"Of course I am," he replied. "With my reputation came responsibility, administrative duties and complications. With them gone, I will be free to teach and do my work out of the public eye: I should have done that from the beginning. Many healers do it, nobody cares about them. They have a private contract with their willing clients who pay them for their time, not the outcome. Once there is a public interest you get pushed into licences and proof and health and safety. It is enough to stop anyone from doing anything worthwhile. The bureaucrats will kill a good thing as a matter of principle. They rather have you die than allow anything they don't understand and cannot prove."

"You know it is ironic," Anuj added. "Jesus was said to have healed people and there are tons of his followers ready to kill you if you don't believe it. Imagine a new messiah coming to earth. They wouldn't burn him at the stake any more, but now they would lock him up for not having a licence."

"That's a bit much, comparing Arpan to Jesus," Erica said.

"You know that isn't what I am trying to do or say," Anuj replied.

"I look forward to be free of all the restrictions again," Arpan said. "I have long come to wish that my fame could be erased, so that I could start from scratch and work with people who appreciate and believe in me. Having been in the limelight only attracted the wrong kind of clientele anyway. This might be a blessing in disguise!"

"You still have a few years before the contract releases you," Anuj pointed out.

"That suits me, too," Arpan said, totally unbroken in his spirit. "I meant to gather a few more disciples and begin my own school. She can't stop me from doing that, especially if I don't involve the elixir."

"Will you still charge all that money?"

"I don't know what to do about that," he said thoughtfully. "I want to give it to a charity but the problem is, once the money is with the charity you cannot simply ask for it back. Like you for example. You came here two years after the treatment and rightfully want to be reimbursed. How could I pay you back if the money had been already spent somewhere in Africa? And how long would I have to wait before I can spend it? Without the right of reimbursement, I will never get a break from the authorities."

"I see."

"And still, by demanding money I became more important and worthy in my client's eyes. If something is free, people don't value it. If their money is paid to charity and my services are effectively free of charge, then it conveys the same message that I don't value my gift or my time and so they don't value it either. I hate such mind games, but they work. Maybe when I reopen my practice I will just leave that part be and trust that my clients will have faith in me."

"It will lessen the commitment," Anuj pointed out. "You always said you needed their complete and full commitment."

"I know what I said but there are many other implications to consider. I will have to find the disciples first and then I will meditate about what to do. The world has changed, and I haven't been participating in it. No wonder I'm not doing a good job at public relations."

"Do you think it was better back in those days than it is now?" Anuj asked. "You were well received 22 years ago."

"We had momentum then, the timing seemed right. I was seeking the publicity, my ego was big, it all contributed to my downfall in the end. I wanted the world to know about my gift and make them believe. Only, people are too busy with themselves these days to care about beliefs and a higher context for their lives, which is why we attracted the wrong kind of people, the ones who thought they could buy their way out of cancer. My gift is not a personal blessing but a blessing for the world. Look what they did with it. How many people tried to stop or destroy me and my reputation? Look at the current witch hunt on alternative healing and the press I got from that darn biography."

"In your new healing centre, will you still administer the elixir?" Erica asked.

"I won't be using it. It is what stands between me and my freedom. They can't measure my energy and my healing, so they'll have to leave that one well alone. The second I use the elixir I become subject to their demands and regulations. I need to break free from all this, find a way to do what I can without being vulnerable."

"They'll find new loopholes in the legislation and stop you," Anuj said disillusioned.

"Then I will have to change strategy again," he said.

175

The next day Erica received the last of her treatments.

"How do you feel it went this time?" she asked him.

"I never treated anyone who had not an actual tumour inside of them. It was a very different experience all the way through last week. I felt the soreness of the spot where they operated."

"But do you think that I am cured now?" she asked timidly.

"You are cured," he assured her. "The money will be transferred to you during the next few days," he added.

"Remember the blessing this time," Anuj said. "Don't throw it away again like last time."

"I will try," she said, and then she walked down the steep hill and all the way to the next village. She took a taxi to the train station and began travelling back to Munich. She picked up a few newspapers at the station and after a long sleep began to read through them. There were some articles about Arpan. It seemed like a planned smear campaign, contesting medical records and questioning the personal experiences. Julia was featured in one of the papers with a picture and a long interview where she described her attempts to bring the elixir to a broader market but could not get Arpan's agreement.

"It gets to show that the man has nothing more to offer to society than a placebo effect at best," the interview went. "Just recently I have become aware of a case where an allegedly healed patient has had her tumour regrow and had to have it surgically removed. She did not have the trust in Arpan to have another healing done by him and decided to go with western medicine instead. That clearly raises a few issues: did she really have cancer the first time round or did the two of them use fake documents to build him up as a miracle worker? If she did have cancer and he *healed* her, then we need to ask ourselves, why did it come back? If he is capable of healing someone at least temporarily then why on earth would she, the beneficiary of his skills before, not try to go back to him? She decided to have surgery, which proves how little even she trusted in his skills. I congratulate the patient on her common sense. Her standard operation was successful and now we can finally say that the patient is clear of cancer, no thanks to Arpan."

Erica nearly ripped the paper apart. So that hateful woman had found out everything and used it to her full advantage. Her return to Munich would prove to be interesting.

Chapter 18

When she got back to her flat in Munich, Erica, as expected, found messages from Julia, but more surprisingly from Gunnar, both asking her to contact them. She kind of figured what Julia would have to say. She would either sack Erica or would promote her, and frankly, Erica could not care less which one it was. She was tired of that woman and could happily wait to find out what her latest mind game was.

Now Gunnar, that was more of a mystery. She sent him a text that she was home and happy to meet with him. He texted her back almost immediately and asked to come to see her that evening at her place.

What is this about?

she asked via text again, before committing to a meeting.

I better tell you in person. All good?

OK. Come at 6.

Gunnar arrived early, with a large bouquet of flowers.

"What's gotten into you?" she asked amused.

"Julia has told me," he said with sweet puppy eyes as he hugged her. "I'm so sorry, I didn't know you had been manipulated by that charlatan. You poor thing, to have your head messed with by some con man like Arpan."

She looked at him bewildered.

"What did Julia tell you exactly?" she asked, removing herself from the embrace and gently pushing him away.

"She said that you thought you had pancreatic cancer because Arpan arranged for a mix up of your medical records. He then took all of your money while pretending to heal you. I don't know how they got you to believe all of this but it explains your behaviour in Prague, hysterical and out of your mind – I can see now that there had to be a reason for it. Nobody can be so out of character."

She stood there with her mouth open, trying to take it all in but Gunnar was in full flow.

"I'm so sorry for all that I said to you," he continued. "You know, my father used to make us children promises he never kept, he drank, forgot things and he would lie to us. He would go to the supermarket and come back, claiming that he had been robbed and beaten, all so that he could spend the grocery money on booze. Sometimes the story would be that he had spent the afternoon cleaning the car of an elderly lady, or helping her change the wheel on her car. It was ridiculous. When we were older we began to ignore him and stopped engaging with him. He didn't like it and he began to make up all kinds of ludicrous stories, just to impress us. He would talk about his achievements at work, that he had met the Swedish Prime Minister on his lunch break and all kind of unbelievably stupid and implausible stories. I don't know why he thought we would believe him or even care but he did. It was hell. When you started talking about a miracle healing I just couldn't take it. It reminded me too much of him and I was suddenly a child again."

Erica just shook her head bewildered. What the hell was he going on about his childhood for?

"But Gunnar, what are you talking about? I did have cancer. There are medical records to prove it," she said.

"Oh dear, he has you believing it still," he said, full of compassion. "Darling, Julia has shown me the entire file. You never had cancer at all. Your records must have been muddled up."

'What!' she thought to herself. Telling Gunnar an implausible story about a medical record mix up; what new kind of deviousness was that woman up to now!

"That's not possible Gunnar. I saw the files, the scans, I was in the hospital room. I had chemo for God's sake. If anyone could *muddle up* medical documents it would be Julia and her minions; it would be easy for *her* to exchange my records for ones that showed no cancer. And it would be a hell of a coincidence if I didn't have cancer two years ago but then suddenly developed pancreatic cancer two years later. This is nonsense," she stated and slammed her fist on the table.

"I know it's a lot to take in," Gunnar said. "You've been taken for a ride and a very good one at that. The power of the mind is enormous. Once you get it in your head that you have cancer, you can develop it. Studies have proven that this is possible and this sad affair shows just how gullible you've been. You've fallen victim to a clever con artist."

"You never met Arpan," she said. "He wouldn't have been able to do that."

"But he could have. He could have had someone working for him in the clinic…"

"Oh Gunnar," she interrupted him, "that is an idiotic idea; besides, Arpan is paying me back all of my money. We can check it now, it might already be in my account. What has he to gain from it?"

"Of course he's paying you back," Gunnar said. "With a law suit looming over his head he better had."

"Whoa! Hang on! What law suit?"

"Julia is taking him to court. Big style. With all of your medical records from then and now, with your bank statements proving how much you paid him to be *cured*. Now that the tumour has returned, he's under a lot of pressure. Maybe he thinks he can buy your silence in court so that you won't testify against him."

"But I spent the last week with Arpan and he never mentioned anything about it," she explained. "When did you launch the law suit?"

"Immediately after I returned from Prague Julia called me into her office. She asked me why you had gone sick and why I had not stayed with you. One thing led to another, you know how persuasive she can be, and before I knew it I had told her everything about your collapse and what I thought then was nothing more than a hysterical cry for attention. She kept pushing me and in the end I told her how you had presented your case."

"How did she react to that? She knew about Arpan, she was in on everything from the start."

"Julia laughed with me about it," he replied. "What else could she have done?"

"She paid him off," Erica insisted. "Her predecessor paid him huge sums of money over twenty years ago to keep him from practising."

Gunnar was visibly shocked at her stubbornness and clearly didn't buy her story. He shook his head but continued:

"Anyway, several days later Julia contacted me again and showed me all of your medical records concerning your initial treatment for the tumour from three years ago. There was no cancer or anything wrong with you."

"That's impossible. I had chemo," she reiterated. "There must be a way of proving that. I was there. There were lots of witnesses for it."

"But that is the point! You were there but you shouldn't have been. You were bizarrely sent a letter with your diagnosis by mistake and the clinic treated the wrong person. There are no other records of you ever having been diagnosed with cancer. They mistakenly treated you with chemo but then you couldn't take the treatment and decided to leave. Add in the fact that you used a false name and you can imagine how it happened. It's a big mess and easy to see why you've become a bit crazy."

She stood there in stunned silence trying to take in what he was saying. It didn't make sense. A medical record mix up! Even if it was true there was no way that Arpan could have engineered it... and then it all suddenly became clear. It was Julia who had arranged the mix up and she had done it to ambush Arpan, to ruin his reputation.

"I'm not having them sue him," she insisted, suddenly wanting to protect her healer. "He's done nothing wrong."

"Well that's between you and Julia," he said, taken aback. "You'll come round to reason when you see the documents and hear Julia out, of that I'm sure. I'm sorry that I judged you so harshly in Prague. Now we can go back to the way we were before then, if you want to."

"No. I don't want to," she said coldly. "I simply don't trust you anymore Gunnar: it's over!"

"You take your time," Gunnar said. "I'll wait. It's a lot to take in all of a sudden and you're clearly too emotional to think straight right now. We had a good thing going, us two."

She took a deep breath and said: "Can't you see that Julia is manipulating my medical history to discredit Arpan?"

"Don't be absurd," Gunnar laughed. "Why on earth would she do that? You can't just go to hospitals and change someone else's history and records. You can be so naïve sometimes."

"Hang on, a minute ago you were accusing Arpan of doing exactly that and now you are saying that it's impossible. You are naïve. If anyone could organise a medical record swap it would be Julia and a pharmaceutical company like ours."

"Now who is naïve? Arpan treated you for a cancerous tumour that the hospital records show you never had. Who do you want to believe now? The hospital can't explain how you got onto those lists to have a CAT scan and receive the chemo, but according to their files you never had cancer. They are launching an investigation to find out how the mix up happened. To think that Julia could have done any of this is nothing but a big conspiracy theory. She had no motive, unless you consider suing an old man for a few pounds a motive. As a scientist, I have learned that the simplest solution is often the right one. A mix up back then explains how you could have been magically *cured* by the conman. The subsequent cancer free results from the private clinic are confirmation that it was never there in the first place."

"Even if all that were to be true," she said slowly, "how do you explain that I got a reoccurrence of exactly the same type of cancer?"

He hesitated fractionally before saying: "It is unbelievable awful of them to make you believe that you had cancer but once they had planted that seed, your mind did the rest for them; it is an amazingly powerful tool. Obsession with cancer can create cancer, but thank God that has been taken care of. I've heard that Julia has paid your bills in the Ukrainian clinic. You see, she's a great friend."

Erica shook her head vehemently. He was merely reciting a well-rehearsed script that Julia had taught him.

"I was ill. I felt terrible the whole time. I had pain and I had chemo. I was off sick from work, I had visitors at the hospital…" she shouted.

"Yes, you were in a hospital but it was a mistake. The symptoms that you were feeling were all psychosomatic, you actually believed that you had a tumour and so you lived all the effects of having one."

"This will never hold in a court of law," she said outraged.

"That's exactly what Julia thinks."

"I need to see her," Erica said and put on her shoes.

"Now? Do you think she's still at the office?" Gunnar asked her with a warm but patronising smile. "I told her I'd be with you tonight and she sends her regards."

"I must find her and get to the bottom of this." Erica spoke with determination.

"What about us?" Gunnar asked. "Are we good?"

"No, I'm sorry but we are far from good. We're from two different worlds. I wish you a good life, Gunnar but you need to leave right now! Goodbye!"

With that, before he knew what had hit him, she forcibly escorted him outside the flat, turned around and slammed the door in his face, leaving him stunned in the immaculate hallway.

Within five minutes she had gotten ready and was in a taxi on the way to the company's office. She had to think quickly. Why had Julia done this? Why had she swapped Erica's medical records? Obviously it was to ruin Arpan but there had to be something else.

She arrived at the huge glass headquarters still trying to process all of the possible scenarios. She found Julia still at her office. A sarcastic smile greeted Erica and an equally acerbic looking secretary appeared out of nowhere and ushered Erica into the meeting room as if she was at school waiting for a reprimand or expulsion. Erica just laughed at the way she was treated like a naughty child instead of the woman who had come here of her own account.

"What on earth do you think you're doing?" Erica jumped straight into the argument as soon as Julia entered. "Who gave you permission to call up all my medical records?"

"You did, my dear, Julia said with a broad grin.

"I never did such a thing," Erica said.

"I beg to differ," came the reply. "How you never came to read the small print in your employment contract is beyond me. Have a good look at the entire medical care plan section and then read the contract you signed with our private health care insurance. I have the right to access everything about you, and so I did."

"Outrageous," Erica hissed. "What about the clinic in Kiev?"

"It seems you signed a document authorizing me there, too," Julia informed her. "Don't look so angry, you should be thanking me. Has it not occurred to you as to why the credit card never charged you for the operation? That's right. We paid for it in full. It's so beneficial to work for a large company who cares. Did you really think you could have afforded this all by yourself, that the quote they gave you in Kiev was a realistic one?"

"How did you manage to swap my original hospital files?" Erica asked, suddenly calm. "I saw the scans, I felt the effects of the tumour; this can't be a mix up of files."

"I'm afraid for you that I didn't swap any files. What you had, back in the day, was probably nothing but trapped wind, the effect of a poor posture and office furniture. We have plenty of witnesses who can attest to your unhealthy and hedonistic lifestyle. It leads to similar complaints like the ones you were experiencing and of course after that, you had the chemo, which took it out of your body. If you want, we can sue the hospital for damages on your behalf. That's how good friends we still are."

"What about my reoccurrence in Prague?" Erica asked. "How did that fit into the picture for you?"

"That was a godsend if there ever was one," Julia said smugly. "I'm so glad you asked, because I've been meaning to gloat about that for weeks."

She looked around the room theatrically and bent down closely to Erica before whispering in her ear.

"Darling, you had an inflamed appendix in Prague. I've never stopped watching you and took action as soon as I heard from the hotel that you were looking for a private clinic. That's how you magically ended up in Dr Adameck's, on a Sunday; he's a close personal friend of mine. I've been dying to tell you this," she added and laughed hysterically. "God, you should see your face, darling. So gullible."

"You really are something else," Erica said, shaking her head in disbelieve. "How did you buy the witnesses?"

"What witnesses?" Julia said amused.

"The doctors, the nurses, etcetera."

"They're all backing our story, or rather, they are backing the truth. All terribly sorry for the ordeal you were put through."

"Why are you doing this?" Erica said, in shock at such hatred and coldness. "Why are you suing Arpan?"

"I need to show up these charlatans and alternative esoteric new age hippy gurus for what they really are. As long as there are people like him promising the moon on a stick, there will be patients who turn down perfectly valid treatment. It's not just our profits that suffer, it's their lives. I need to set an example, drag someone like Arpan through the mud and teach him a lesson about how he is messing with people's hopes and ultimately, their existence."

"Or are you trying to blackmail him into giving you the formula of the elixir?"

"Ah… finally… you've caught on," Julia said smiling. "Such a deal would certainly make me more agreeable. If only he wasn't so stubborn."

"Let me talk to him. Maybe I can persuade him," Erica said.

"He's turned us down time and time again," Julia said. "You'll be wasting your energy."

"I spent the last week with him, Julia," Erica said triumphantly. "I have a handle on this, I reckon."

For the first time since the meeting had started, Julia looked less sure of herself. "How did you see him? I had a GPS tracking on your phone and you were in Munich the entire time."

"I never took the phone with me," Erica gloated. "I travelled with cash and took a scenic route. I am so glad that paid off."

"And you think Arpan is ready to sell the elixir if I drop the court charges?" Julia said, suddenly business-like and very eager.

"He isn't bothered about the law suit," Erica told her. "He didn't mention it once during that entire time. He, too, wants his reputation ruined to put an end to all this media interest and the public attention. Dropping the law suit is my fee for brokering the deal. If I read the situation correctly, Arpan would have different conditions."

"If he is ready to sell the elixir then I'm sure we could come to some mutually beneficial arrangement," Julia said, very excited. "I'll get the company helicopter ready right now."

"Hang on," Erica demanded. "Before that happens, you and I are going to a Notary Office and sign legally binding documents in front of independent witnesses. Until then I'm not going to do anything. I don't trust you as far as I can throw you."

Julia smiled smugly. "Fair enough. I shall have you picked up by a company car tomorrow at seven a.m."

Julia stood by her word and the following morning signed a simple and straightforward agreement giving Erica the guarantees and reassurances she had asked for, then the two of them boarded the company helicopter and made their way to Wales.

Arpan and Anuj were visibly surprised to see Erica by the gate. She had told Julia to wait in the car that had brought them from the airfield.

"What brings you back so soon?" Anuj asked.

"I've heard about the law suit coming your way and I need to warn you. Julia has gotten hold of all of my records and she has probably falsified a few, too. They now show that I have never had cancer and so she can easily discredit you, she may even have sufficient evidence to put you in prison."

"I don't really care about that," Arpan said. "Let her do her worst. She'll do that anyway."

"I can make it go away for you," Erica said, looking him squarely in the eye. "Now is the time to sell the elixir to her and everything will be over. You said yourself that you're ready to move on and start a new life, one as teacher and a healer out of the limelight."

"Hmmn… and her law suit will discredit me perfectly and I get exactly what I want," Arpan pointed out. "Without realising it, she's actually doing me a favour."

"If Hilda only knew what trouble her introducing us has caused." Erica said. "I wonder where she is now."

"Hilda is fine. She's on Grand Cayman Island having the time of her life on Julia's pay-out. She won't be bothered by any of this."

"How do you know?"

"Well… our mutual friends sometimes talk", he said cheerfully.

"You were not going to use the elixir again anyway," Erica persisted, feeling that she was close to getting him to agree. "With the law suit you will remain on the radar – you'll never have an easy life. Think of the money you can make from Julia; that elixir is worth many millions."

"It's not worth anything," Anuj interjected.

"25 years of worldwide exclusive usage, sub contracts and licences for cancer research institutions all over the world: this is a gold mine. You could have a rocket built to fly you to Venus and back with the money, don't you get it?" Erica said. "You could build a school in every city of the world and run multiple top charities with it. You should have done this a long time ago."

"You still don't get it, do you?" Arpan said. "The elixir alone is useless."

"I know," Erica said. "I know it and you know it too, but Julia doesn't. She believes you're just making that healing part of the treatment up and the elixir, this compound that you've stumbled across, is really the important part. If it doesn't fully work then there is no harm done; it'll cost her a fortune, but maybe they can work on your formula, find the active compound and use it, making it effective without your magic."

"I doubt that," Arpan said and went quiet, appearing to consider carefully what she had said. Just when Erica had given up hope, he finally said: "But you're right. This is probably a good time to give it all up. Get Julia here to make the deal. It's time to move on to my new endeavours."

The next few days seemed like a blur to Erica. Julia moved quickly; she didn't drive a hard bargain for the elixir and offered a colossal sum for it. All that she asked for was the certificate that Arpan once got by the independent expert who had testified that the elixir was harmless. At a Notary Office in Munich, Arpan and the expert handed over the documents to Julia who eagerly arranged for a bank transfer.

"For the record I would like to state in front of all of these witnesses here that the elixir was never used on its own, but only in combination with my healing powers," Arpan said. "Should you fail to make it work on its own the risk is entirely yours."

"Yes, yes," Julia said impatiently. "As long as this is the exact formula you've always been using I don't care about your pathetic claims."

"This is it," the independent witness confirmed.

"No hard feelings?" Julia said to Arpan and stretched out her hand to seal the deal.

"None at all," he replied and gave her his hand.

Julia didn't waste any more time with pleasantries but took off with her entourage right away.

"There she goes," Anuj said with a broad grin. "She'll have a rude awakening soon enough."

"Are you totally sure that it won't work without you?" Erica asked.

"Absolutely," Arpan said.

Erica shook her head. "I am sure she will make it work and it will revolutionise cancer treatment."

Arpan turned his head slowly towards her, looked her squarely in the eye and said: "Erica, what I gave her is saline solution; my famous elixir is nothing but a slightly modified and coloured saline solution."

"I beg your pardon?" she whispered.

"All healers need a ritual," he explained. "Wherever I went in my search for a healing power, every teacher had their own ritual, be it a prayer, a mantra, a gesture or a sequence of hand movements to focus, to invoke their powers. I haven't come across one healer who didn't have something like it. As the student being taught by all these wonderful men and women, I found comfort in these rituals and I decided that if I were ever start to practice healing, I would need something similar. Initially, I used symbols similar to ones used in Reiki but it seemed a cheap rip off. When I decided to work in the UK, where so many people would be sceptical, I made up this harmless elixir to appeal to the more rational clients, the ones who were still thinking of western medicine as superior. Giving them a part of the treatment that was oddly familiar from hospitals helped them to take me and my work more seriously. Reproducing the same colour for every solution was the most difficult thing, something that you noticed and nearly caught us out on."

"So it was all a trick?" Erica asked, half outraged and half full of schadenfreude for Julia.

"No. It was a prop to make the entire experience more palatable for some of the clients," Arpan said.

"Julia will be apoplectic with rage," Erica laughed. "Are you not worried she will sue you?"

"Not after she discredited me publicly in the newspapers. She will never be able to tell anyone that she made a deal with me after all. After what she said about me and my elixir in the paper, especially just recently, she could never acknowledge it, or her reputation and that of the company would go down the drain. She has manoeuvred herself into a corner and there is no way out of it."

"She has certainly done that," Erica got out, through the continued fit of laughter. "Now you must give Hilda my love when you see or speak to her next."

"I will do that," Arpan said. "We're leaving on a plane tomorrow morning to see her. We're actually moving to the Grand Cayman Islands ourselves."

"What an odd choice," Erica said. "Sounds almost like you're on the run from the law."

"In a way that is the case," Anuj said. "They don't have the same laws about healing and licences as they do here in Europe. It is as good a place as any to start our training school. Thanks to Julia's over generous cheque we can have our new recruits flown in from all over the globe to where we are. Hilda has done all the groundwork for us, we will be undisturbed there."

"Congratulations," Erica said. "I'm glad things have worked out.

"You must come and visit us sometime," Anuj offered.

"I'll be sure to do that."

"What will you do next?" Arpan asked her.

"Julia has given me six months off as a thank you for brokering the deal. I doubt she will want me back when she finds out that your elixir is useless," Erica said, still struggling to suppress a giggle. "Now that I'll get my money back from you, I will probably take a long holiday in Greece. I've always wanted to do that and then I will have to look for a new job."

Epilogue

Erica sat in a white treatment room in the private health clinic that had first treated her when she had been diagnosed with cancer. She had scheduled an appointment with the doctor who had arranged for her course of chemo therapy.

"Mrs Whittaker, or Mrs Miller, how would you like me to address you?" her doctor asked. Although in his fifties he was of a nervous disposition, always moving, full of energy, friendly but slippery.

"Whittaker, please."

"Let me pre-empt this discussion by saying that we are willing to pay substantial damages to you, especially if we could settle our dispute out of the limelight of court and the press," he said without looking into her eyes. "How do you feel about that?"

"I'm open to suggestions but I'm primarily here to satisfy my own curiosity. I would really like to see the documents in question, the two files that were mixed up?"

"Well, that is of course the embarrassing part for me," he said. "Is that really necessary?"

"Yes, for my peace of mind it is rather essential," she replied.

"One moment please, I will get my assistant to get those files for you."

Shortly afterwards Erica was looking at two sets of X-rays and scan results.

"You see, it is particularly shameful for me," said the doctor. "If you compare the two files closely it's easy to identify the differences in body stature between the two patients. How I could have looked at these cancer-riddled scans and not have realised that they could not relate to you, I can't understand: this makes me look highly unprofessional."

Erica opened her bag and got out her set of scans from the other private clinic.

"These are scans I had made a few years ago," she explained. "I'm just trying to see which one of these they match."

He examined the files she had brought with her and compared them with his X-rays.

"These are a perfect match," he said.

She looked at them startled. She ripped the documents out of his hands and looked at them unable to process what she was seeing. Her X-rays matched the cancer free X-rays from the hospital, not the cancer riddled ones.

"There must be another mix up," she said.

"Impossible," he replied. Look at those dates, look at the body frame. These are both yours. Again, I'm so sorry to have put you through the ordeal of chemo. I was going through a difficult divorce at the time, I have no idea how all of this could have happened to me. I sincerely hope you are willing to meet us half way as far as compensation is concerned..."

She hardly heard him as he waffled on and on about how much pressure he had been under. This couldn't be right. She really never had had cancer; Julia had been telling the truth all along. No! No! No! This couldn't be right.

Suddenly, she snapped back into reality, her subconscious picking up on something that he had just said. What had he just said about his wife? Something about the Grand Cayman Islands?

"I'm sorry. Can you say that last part again, about Grand Cayman Island?" she asked.

"Since the divorce my wife lives on the Grand Cayman Island but I mustn't bore you with my private life," he said quickly. "I apologise."

"Hold on!" she said. "Hold on! Tell me, what's your wife's name?" Erica asked.

"Hilda."

The End

Thanks

A big thank you to my sister Susanne, without whose critique, I would never have published this novel.

Thanks to Dr Kelly MacDonald who helped me with the medical side of the plot by answering my many questions so patiently and thoroughly. If there are any technical errors in the novel they are of course entirely my fault, not hers.

Thanks to my editor Wanda Hartzenberg, a wonderful muse for many writers, for being a friend and for believing in me and to my early readers: Brenda Perlin and Susan Tarr for helping to find many numerous tpyos.

Thanks to my amazing friend and cover designer Daz Smith for getting it right once again and for pushing me into publishing in the first place.

Last, but not least, to Ryan for his never ending patience and support.

Did you like the book?

Let everyone know by posting a review on Goodreads, Amazon.com or Amazon.co.uk to tell others about it.

More books by Christoph Fischer:

The Luck of the Weissensteiners (Three Nations Trilogy: Book 1)

In the sleepy town of Bratislava in 1933 the daughter of a Jewish weaver falls for a bookseller from Berlin, Wilhelm Winkelmeier. Greta Weissensteiner seemingly settles in with her in-laws but the developments in Germany start to make waves in Europe and re-draw the visible and invisible borders. The political climate, the multi-cultural jigsaw puzzle of the disintegrating Czechoslovakian state and personal conflicts make relations between the couple and the families more and more complex. The story follows the families through the war with its predictable and also its unexpected turns and events and the equally hard times after. What makes The Luck of the Weissensteiners so extraordinary is the chance to consider the many different people who were never in concentration camps, never in the military, yet who nonetheless had their own indelible Holocaust experiences. This is a wide-ranging, historically accurate exploration of the connections between social status, personal integrity and, as the title says, luck.

Praise for The Luck of the Weissensteiners: "… powerful, engaging, you cannot remain untouched…" "Fischer deftly weaves his tapestry of history and fiction, with a grace…"

On Amazon: http://smarturl.it/Weissensteiners
On Goodreads: http://bit.ly/12Rnup8
On Facebook: http://on.fb.me/1bua395
Trailer: http://studio.stupeflix.com/v/OtmyZh4Dmc
B&N: http://ow.ly/Btvas

Sebastian
(Three Nations Trilogy: Book 2)

Sebastian is the story of a young man who has his leg amputated before World War I. When his father is drafted to the war it falls on to him to run the family grocery store in Vienna, to grow into his responsibilities, bear loss and uncertainty and hopefully find love. Sebastian Schreiber, his extended family, their friends and the store employees experience the 'golden days' of pre-war Vienna, the times of the war and the end of the Monarchy while trying to make a living and to preserve what they hold dear. Fischer convincingly describes life in Vienna during the war, how it affected the people in an otherwise safe and prosperous location, the beginning of the end for the Monarchy, the arrival of modern thoughts and trends, the Viennese class system and the end of an era. As in the first part of the trilogy, "The Luck of The Weissensteiners" we are confronted again with themes of identity, Nationality and borders. The step back in time made from Book 1 and the change of location from Slovakia to Austria enables the reader to see the parallels and the differences deliberately out of the sequential order. This helps to see one not as the consequence of the other, but to experience them as the momentary reality as it must have felt for the people at the time.

Praise for Sebastian: "I fell in love with Sebastian...a truly inspiring read for anyone!!!!" – "This is a MUST read, INTELLIGENT, SENSITIVE, ENGAGING, PERFECT."

On Amazon: http://smarturl.it/TNTSeb
On Goodreads: http://ow.ly/pthHZ
On Facebook: http://ow.ly/pthNy
Trailer: http://studio.stupeflix.com/v/95jvSpHf5a/
B&N: http://ow.ly/Btvbw

The Black Eagle Inn
(Three Nations Trilogy: Book 3)

The Black Eagle Inn is an old established Restaurant and Farm business in the sleepy Bavarian countryside outside of Heimkirchen. Childless Anna Hinterberger has fought hard to make it her own and keep it running through WWII. Religion and rivalry divide her family as one of her nephews, Markus has got her heart and another nephew, Lukas has got her ear. Her husband Herbert is still missing and for the wider family life in post-war Germany also has some unexpected challenges in store.

Once again Fischer tells a family saga with war in the far background and weaves the political and religious into the personal. Being the third in the Three Nations Trilogy this book offers another perspective on war, its impact on people and the themes of nations and identity.

On Amazon: http://smarturl.it/TBEI
On Goodreads: http://ow.ly/pAX8G
On Facebook: http://ow.ly/pAX3y
Trailer: http://studio.stupeflix.com/v/mB2JZUuBaI/

Time to Let Go

Time to Let Go is a contemporary family drama set in Britain. Following a traumatic incident at work Stewardess Hanna Korhonen decides to take time off work and leaves her home in London to spend quality time with her elderly parents in rural England. There she finds that neither can she run away from her problems, nor does her family provide the easy getaway place that she has hoped for. Her mother suffers from Alzheimer's disease and, while being confronted with the consequences of her issues at work, she and her entire family are forced to reassess their lives.

The book takes a close look at family dynamics and at human nature in a time of a crisis. Their challenges, individual and shared, take the Korhonens on a journey of self-discovery and redemption.

On Amazon: http://smarturl.it/TTLG
On Goodreads: http://ow.ly/BtKs7
On Facebook: http://ow.ly/BtKtQ

Conditions

When Charles and Tony's mother dies the estranged brothers must struggle to pick up the pieces, particularly so given that one of them is mentally challenged and the other bitter about his place within the family.

The conflict is drawn out over materialistic issues, but there are other underlying problems which go to the heart of what it means to be part of a family which, in one way or another. has cast one aside.

Prejudice, misconceptions and the human condition in all forms feature in this contemporary drama revolving around a group of people who attend the subsequent funeral at the British South Coast.

Meet flamboyant gardener Charles, loner Simon, selfless psychic Elaine, narcissistic body-builder Edgar, Martha and her version of unconditional love and many others as they try to deal with the event and its aftermath.

On Amazon: http://smarturl.it/CONDITIONSCFF
On Goodreads: http://ow.ly/
On Facebook: http://ow.ly/C0ZqX

A Short Biography

Christoph Fischer was born in Germany, near the Austrian border, as the son of a Sudeten-German father and a Bavarian mother. Not a full local in the eyes and ears of his peers, he developed an ambiguous sense of belonging and home in Bavaria. He moved to Hamburg in pursuit of his studies and to lead a life of literary indulgence. After a few years he moved on to the UK where he now lives in a small hamlet, not far from Bath. He and his partner have three Labradoodles to complete their family.

Christoph worked for the British Film Institute, in libraries, museums and for an airline. 'The Luck of The Weissensteiners' was published in November 2012; 'Sebastian' in May 2013 and The Black Eagle Inn in October 2013. These three historical novels form the 'Three Nations Trilogy'. 'Time to Let Go' was published in May 2014 and 'Conditions' in October 2014. He has written several other novels which are in the later stages of editing and finalisation.

For further information you can follow him on:

Twitter:
https://twitter.com/CFFBooks
Pinterest:
http://www.pinterest.com/christophffisch/
Google +:
https://plus.google.com/u/0/106213860775307052243
LinkedIn:
https://www.linkedin.com/profile/view?id=241333846
Blog:
http://writerchristophfischer.wordpress.com
Website:
www.christophfischerbooks.com
Facebook:
www.facebook.com/WriterChristophFischer

Made in the USA
Columbia, SC
29 May 2017